The Real Sleeper

Also by
Theodore Roosevelt Gardner II

The Paper Dynasty
Off the Wall
Something Nice to See
Lotusland

The Real Sleeper

By
Theodore Roosevelt Gardner II

A love story

ALLEN A. KNOLL, PUBLISHERS
Santa Barbara, CA

Library of Congress Cataloging-in-Publication Data

Gardner, Theodore Roosevelt.
    The real sleeper : a love story / by Theodore Roosevelt Gardner,
II.
        p.   cm.
    ISBN 0-9627297-8-7 (alk. paper)
    I. Title.
    PS3557.A7146R4   1995
    813'.54--dc20   95-36080
                                                         CIP

Typeface is electra old style face, 12 point
Printed on 60-pound Booktext natural acid-free paper
3-piece case bound with Roxite B and Kivar 9, Smyth Sewn

It don't mean a thing
If it ain't got that swing.
 —*Irving Mills*

EDGAR

I used to flatter myself that I was a late bloomer. Now that I am on a collision course with eternity, I have come to realize it is entirely possible that I have not bloomed at all. Maybe I'm one of those plants that blooms then dies, but whose blooms are spectacular, ten- to fifteen-feet tall and bursting with color. I think the bloom would be worth it.

What I thought would never fail me had

failed me. The mechanisms of my hyperactive passion were flagging. I was developing a real fear of the "I" word: Impotence!

My father liked to recite a poem in this regard:

> *From twenty to thirty, if a man lives right,*
> *It's once in the morning and once at night.*
> *From thirty to forty, if he still lives right,*
> *He gives up the morning, but keeps the night.*
> *From forty to fifty he's at his peak,*
> *But that other stuff is once a week.*
> *From fifty to sixty he still has a yen,*
> *But statistics show it's now and then.*
> *From sixty to seventy he will find*
> *Whatever he does is all in his mind.*

Sixty was staring me in the face like an avenging angel, and I thought if I didn't do something about it, God would turn me into a pillar of saltpeter.

Then a miracle happened.

And I don't believe in miracles.

I met the most gorgeous woman, *young* woman, I had ever seen. And no sooner had we met than she took her clothes off, whereupon we chatted away like we were the best of friends.

Lovers even.

We weren't lovers, of course, but afterwards I couldn't get Kelly O'Leary out of my mind. It was a pleasant obsession at first, then, before I knew what happened, my passion became debilitating.

I was in serious need of therapy, but I didn't have a lot of faith in psychiatry, nor could I afford it.

So I painted her—from her promotional brochure. I painted her likeness so often, I developed a queasy vertigo, like I imagine a real good case of seasickness would be. Of course, I wouldn't know about that. I've never had the spirit of adventure required to take a sea voyage.

First I drew her in pencil with her clothes on, then with her clothes off, as I had seen her. Then I tried paint. First watercolor, then oil. Easier to paint over your flops with oil. I worked long hours at my easel. Hours became days. I was obsessed. Possessed. Like Handel composing his _Messiah_. But I got this aggravating dizziness because I couldn't capture her spirit.

I have been drawing and painting for almost thirty years. It's fun—and now I tried it as therapy.

I listened to classical music while I painted, and the music affected my work. Beethoven's *bam, bam, boom* gave me bold, Rouault-like strokes; Mozart's *deedle deedle, dum* caused a more delicate approach, like Renaissance line drawing. Debussy's *whooee woosh* and I was in my Impressionist mode. Even the smell of the oils changed with the music. A hearty stew for Beethoven, crustless finger sandwiches for Mozart, and for Debussy a pasta primavera.

I had come home to find a note on the kitchen table:

> *Edgar:*
> > *Off to convention in Atlanta.*
> *Ethel asked me to fill in for her*
> *at last minute — flu or something.*
> *Back Tuesday p.m. Hope you*
> *can make do.*
> > *Penelope*

Yes, I could make do. Solitude was more and more appealing. Having the run of the house, listening to the refrigerator hum, not answering the phone, listening to Penelope's messages coming in on her answering machine, eating at odd hours when the mood struck me.

Outside it could have been sunny or raining for all I knew. I had a window, but I had not been looking out of it. The phone rang. I didn't answer it. It would've been my mother or Penelope. I would call my mother later. Penelope would call back. My mind was only on my work. It was so all-consuming, yet so unsatisfactory, it was making me physically ill.

I gave up writing thirty-some years ago under the burden of a suffocating pile of rejection slips. I couldn't even get my wife to read my manuscripts. I once saw a *New Yorker* cartoon I thought personified my literary relationship with my wife, Penelope. A woman is seated with a manuscript on her lap. She speaks to her expectant husband standing by:

"Well—and I'm not just saying this because you're my husband—it stinks."

So I turned to painting. You can flash a painting in front of someone and have their reaction in seconds. Write a book and you are asking for a major time commitment from people who aren't always prone to give it.

"Fame is the spur," someone once said, but I no longer feel it in my flesh. I don't really care if anyone sees my paintings. I just like painting them. The joy is in the journey sort of thing.

I gave up trying to capture Kelly on canvas, so all I had left was words. Maybe then, I thought, I could understand why I was so crazy about her when everything was absolutely against it. I mean *everything*, including age, background, education, economic class and marital status.

I read in one of those gratuitous publications that middle age is from forty-five to sixty, so I was on the verge of slipping to the next pigeon-hole in life. The one where I could look forward to lower movie admissions and lower back pains.

Kelly barely graduated from high school and I almost got my Ph.D. (my thesis in Class Distinctions Manifested in the Works of Francis Scott Key Fitzgerald). I am the product of a middle-class home, she of a single, uneducated mother.

Seeing Kelly nude reminded me the female body is a thing of surpassing beauty, sinuous and sensuous, the like of which we are not liable to see. What can you think of that begins to approach it? A well-designed teapot? A sports car? A chaise lounge?

I have been married thirty-five years without ever experiencing reciprocal physical passion. Now that I am within striking distance of a senior discount at the Home Improvement Center and selected movie theaters, I've decided I want that experience before I can no longer do what is necessary to experience it.

Already, I've got pain from arthritis which seems to hopscotch from one joint to another. I get winded putting on my socks—having to surmount an excessive midsection in reaching my feet doesn't make it any easier.

But when I put on a suit—one of the newer, larger sizes—I'm presentable enough. The hair is white, sure, but swept back with a brush it looks, if not dashing or sexy, distinguished. You could say I have strong bones. At my best, I look like one of those plastic surgeons who can do a half-dozen tucks a day, bank his twenty thou in fees and still have time for a round of golf before sunset.

My financial status is considerably more modest, but I flatter myself thinking you can't tell it by looking at me.

What I've come to think of as my passion-predicament might strike you as a little surprising when you consider my background.

My father was a ribald dentist. My mother, I always thought, was put upon by the ribald dentist. Later I realized she could not only hold her own but maybe even take credit for some of the Doc's more colorful reactions.

Edgar

At home we called him "the Doc." His dental assistants called him "Doctor." Not "*the* doctor," not "Dr. Wellington," but simply "Doctor." Still, today, if I hear "Doctor will see you now," I get irritated. My vague sense is that "Doctor" without the article connotes oneness, singularity, like "God will see you now." There is no messing with the one almighty and omnipotent God. If *He* will see you, you are mighty lucky indeed, unless, perhaps, he is seeing you to welcome you over to His camp.

And these God-sayers who deify their employer (and their Lothario for all I know) unhesitatingly call me "Ed." No one else in my life has called me that. But the one God must give them the license to belittle the rest of us.

"Doctor will see you now, Ed." Not "Jack will see you, Mr. Wellington."

My mother called my father "God" a couple times, but I never heard her call him "Doctor." "The Doc" was as far as she would go.

I'll never forget when Doctor laid the facts of life on me. He did it with such exuberance, such panache. None of this handing me a book with crude drawings, none of this "You know it all already," none of this drunken slurring veiled mystery about "privates." No, the Doc went right for the jugular. "It's the greatest thing in the world, son, if you do it right. It's more than a mingling of genitalia, it's simply the greatest thing in life—a mystical thrill beyond anything else you will ever experience. You find a girl who turns up her nose at it, you head for the hills without her as fast as you can.

"You'll find plenty who pooh-pooh it, son, and all I can say when you run up against one of those thin-lipped virgins with a stone heart that pumps ice water, is run for your life. Don't under any circumstances saddle yourself with one, no matter how *nice* she seems, no matter how beautiful she is, no matter how rich—nothing else will matter if you don't have that mystical connection—that greatest of all natural forces. You know what the man said: 'It don't mean a thing if it ain't got that swing.' And by God, that's right on the money."

I can still see him standing over me at the kitchen table. The Doc was a man of commanding flamboyance. He was not a word mincer. But I also sensed, even at twelve, that he was hopelessly enslaved to hyperbole. All his admonitions about the superiority of sex left me feeling that he was denigrating my mother, whom I not *only* loved, but pitied.

For the great ebullient Doc didn't spend a lot of time at home with Mother. I became the substitute husband, squiring her to this charity event and that picnic; all obligatory affairs attended while the Doc was conducting his own affairs.

So I ignored his advice. And, of course, I regret it.

There were unspoken undercurrents there. Even at my tender age, I felt the Doc was telling me my mother didn't "do it right" and his dental assistants did, or they moved on to chaster pastures. And the women patients with the past-due bills that were never sent out for collection, they surely did it right.

I have never given up trying to "do it right." But up until now, one of the overriding ironies of my life has been while I aspired to be like my father, I wound up more like my mother. While I longed for his libidinous flamboyance, his aura of command, I became repressed and mildly subjugated to a major breadwinner.

Perhaps it was because of my sympathy for my mother, perhaps not, but I was severely retarded in my interaction with the complementary sex.

Until, as I said, I met Kelly.

KELLY AND EDGAR

She wandered into the photography studio looking like one of those Dickens kids who is about to ask for more food.

In one hand the waif held a blonde, floozie wig, in the other a black notebook which was her portfolio.

She was all in oyster white, not quite the conceit of pure white. Under an open corduroy shirt, a tee shirt; below all that a pair of sawed-off denims through which poked bare legs terminating in sneakers. The sneakers, which took her to and fro, were virgin white.

Her hair was short, wispy black, and she had an Irish name, though she looked Italian.

The earthquake had taken a chunk out of the Santa Monica Freeway at the stop next to the studio. The cars were backed up at the Robertson exit, but the model had taken another route. When she came in, she looked frightened. "Those gang boys scared me to death," she said to no one in particular. "I wanted to ask directions, but I was scared to stop."

She had a breezy Southern lilt to her voice, like a wisteria dropping its flowers. She claimed to be from some backwater in Oregon, but it didn't seem to fit her.

She said, "Hi," to Gary the photographer and Jake the male model. After an uncomfortable silence, Edgar introduced himself to her.

She smiled. "I'm Kelly O'Leary," she said, taking his hand, and looking at him like a jeweler inspecting a flawed gemstone.

Edgar shook her hand and swallowed some air. The waif was twenty-three. Edgar was fifty-nine and seven-twelfths, give or take a couple days.

Kelly's clothes were off-putting androgynous. Between the sockless shoes and the edge of the corduroy shirt, Kelly's legs were thin, almost shapeless supports for a body that didn't seem to need much support.

Edgar had requested a thinnish model for the book cover—not too buxom, not too glamorous. Like the girl next door—who never looked as good as you thought she had. But looking at Kelly O'Leary in oyster white, he wondered if she had any body at all.

The studio looked like the backstage of a small theater—overhead lights, a curtain flying from the tall ceiling. The most striking thing to Edgar was the white wall that curved down into the floor so you wouldn't see any corners on the pictures shot there. It could look, if you liked, as if you were standing in the Gobi Desert.

Gary was dancing around the lights and umbrellas, adjusting and turning. He was a squarish young man in a faded blue tee shirt, with facial hair that appeared to be sprouting randomly.

The male model, a well-constructed man with picture-book handsomeness, was dressed in a sweater and khakis. He would keep his clothes on for the shoot.

Kelly slipped into the small bathroom to ladle on the makeup and put the floozie wig in place. Edgar couldn't take his eyes off her—she had not closed the door.

When she came out of the bathroom, she showed Edgar her book. "This is my portfolio," she said, and handed it to him. There was the twinkle of pride in her voice.

In the center of the book were two pages of nude shots. Edgar was amazed at how startlingly beautiful this Dickens waif looked, courtesy of glamour photography. In a pocket on the inside of the back cover, he found a W-2 IRS form showing the prior year to have yielded Kelly O'Leary a gross income of $6,400 and change.

Kelly had drifted off to say something to the photographer, but returned as Edgar was closing the portfolio.

"Here," she said, taking the portfolio, "did you see these?" She turned to the nudes. "He's just the best photographer. He's famous!"

She had such pride in her voice, Edgar was caught off guard. Embarrassed, he quickly closed the book and said, "Very nice," with no particular emphasis.

Their eyes met with a flash of understanding. Edgar was blushing and she, the offspring of a less constrained time, was amused, but sympathetic. She found Edgar's embarrassment cute.

Hers was a different kind of achievement than his. No doubt pictures would be added to her portfolio as time went on, even this book cover they were shooting today. But in time the additions would ritardando, then stop. Bodies have a way of selling us out. Then she would have to make choices, and the choices wouldn't be between medicine, law and architecture.

Gary set the stage with his models. Kelly was to be photographed front and back nude while Jake read a newspaper on a park bench. Shadows from the leaves of the trees were to shade her sexual characteristics from the squeamish.

The book cover had been Edgar's boss' idea; an experiment to see if they could sell a few more books.

It took Gary hours to set up the lights and to make the leaves shade just the right places.

"Shall I get nude?" Kelly asked after an hour.

"Not yet," Gary said.

Since high school, Kelly had supported herself for five years without working in an office.

"Do you enjoy your work?" Edgar asked her.

"Why, yes, I do," she said. "I could *never* do a nine-to-five job, I mean, I just couldn't. That would drive me crazy."

"It must be a hard go."

"Well, yes, it is sometimes. Some weeks I'll go out on five interviews a day and get only three jobs a week."

"That sounds good to me," Edgar said.

"That's if I'm lucky," she said. "I didn't go to college," she added.

The models were on the floor area they used for the set. Edgar was in a chair off to one side of the camera. The models were well lighted–everything else in the windowless room was dark.

Kelly put her arms under her tee shirt and seemed to caress herself and Edgar got his first glimpse of her delicately formed breasts. They were just so perfect for the cover; he was relieved that there was something under the androgynous shirt. She had a kind of beauty that, naturally coupled with innocence, made him want to protect her from harm.

They exchanged a lot of glances in that photo session, and whenever their eyes met she would smile, the most perfect smile Edgar had ever seen. His wife, Penelope, was not a smiler so this was new to him.

"We're ready," Gary finally announced.

"Oh," Kelly was excited, "shall I get nude?"

"Yes."

"Oooo," Kelly said, already on her way to the empty chair next to Edgar, where she crouched down and started to take off her shoes.

"You can keep the shoes on," Gary said. "We're only getting you from the knees up."

"Oh, good," she said, lifting her tee shirt. She dropped the shorts and bikini panties with the most guileless abandon and threw them on the chair.

How foolish he was to have worried about Kelly's body, Edgar thought. It was hard to imagine how it could have been better. Of all the times he had imagined young girls getting out of their clothing, he never thought it could be so quick and graceful at the same time.

Edgar's heart stopped dead as he watched her move into position; then she turned to face the camera—and him—in a liquid motion, with the grace of a ballerina.

She seemed a new person standing before the three men. It was as though her status among them had suddenly been exalted. She was center stage, the focus of their attention and lust, and she couldn't have been happier about it.

While Gary was adjusting the shadows and taking Polaroids, the male model continually stole glances at the parts of Kelly that were customarily hidden from view.

Suddenly Edgar felt the contrast of the stark-naked girl (except for the sneakers, of course) and the rest of them, covered from head to toe with superfluous layers of goods. He felt a gnawing embarrassment. Here he was to supervise a nude photo session—to see that the photographer got it the way they wanted it—and he didn't want Kelly to show her body to these other two men.

Edgar wanted to shout, "Don't look!" His face was red with pent-up anxiety. He found Kelly's eyes, and had the strange sense she was trying to reassure him that everything was all right.

The Real Sleeper

As if to prove it, she began chattering away as though it were the most normal thing in the world to talk to three clothed men while the lone woman was stark naked.

She was so beautiful—physically perfect. Edgar could picture girls like Kelly from his high school days. They would be on the sidelines at the dances, in the little cliques he could never penetrate, chewing gum and wearing blue jeans. Edgar never had a pair of blue jeans.

He spent most of his time that day trying to concoct some way to ask her out without seeming ridiculous. He was naked between the ears. It had been almost forty years since he had asked a girl out, and that had been so traumatic. He remembered his first attempt at college. He had worked in the bookstore and this intriguing-looking natural blonde came in. She was attractive, but not in the "pretty" sense. She had a sphinx-like countenance upon her and Edgar was the lucky one who got to wait on her. He dragged the procedure out as long as he could and before she left, he had pocketed her name and address.

He checked her schedule in the student administration center. Today he imagined security fears would make this information inaccessible, but then it was there and he took advantage of it.

Edgar waited outside her classroom. His heart was pumping him up for a sprint. She arrived at the last minute. He stepped out in front of her, hoping she would remember him.

"Hi," he gulped, "I'm Edgar Wellington —would you go to the dance with me?"

She stared at him, Miss Sphinx. His heart went nuts. "Do I know you?" she asked, and he had to say she was haughty.

"No, but I'd like to get to know you," he said, and she marched into the room without the blessing of another word.

Asking Kelly out would be no easier for Edgar now than it would have been forty years ago.

Suddenly he blurted, "I appreciate your doing this. Thanks for coming."

"Thanks for having us," Kelly said. Edgar felt a warmth in that very nice instinct on Kelly's part. It didn't seem so important that she probably didn't know who Zola was. Maybe she even thought Baudelaire was some kind of beer.

"I don't have any social life," Kelly was saying to Jake. She spoke with the abandon of an alert adolescent. "I don't have time. I'm always out on an interview, a reading, or a shoot, and I'm in bed at seven o'clock most of the time."

"Seven? At night?" Edgar asked her.

"Yeah," Kelly said. "My roommate goes to bed at seven. It's a small place so I don't stay up."

"How long do you sleep? I mean, do you get up at five?"

"In the *morning*, you mean? Oh, no. I can sleep *forever*. I'll sleep till noon sometimes."

"Really?"

"Oh, yeah, I love it," she enthused. "You know, it's funny how sometimes you can't stay awake at night, you just fall off to sleep? Sometimes I just can't stay awake no matter what. But I *never* can't stay asleep. I never feel like, well, I just have this uncontrollable thing about getting awake. I'm a real sleeper."

Edgar started to wonder what it must be like for a young girl to make a living selling her beauty. Kelly, and others like her, must traipse from office to office, dragging an upbeat, sunny disposition, enthusiastic but not pushy, eager but not desperate, pleasing but not seductive. It must be a delicate balancing act to get everything just right. But the salesmanship is indispensable.

Kelly and Edgar

Imagine the thick skin the girls must develop to ward off the high incidence of rejection. No wonder Kelly went to bed at seven.

Suddenly Edgar realized Kelly had a beautifully tan-toned body, without any tan lines.

"How do you get such an even tan?" Edgar asked.

"I tan in the nude."

Edgar didn't miss a word from her. She spoke to the photographer, Edgar listened. She spoke to the male model on the set, he picked it all up.

"No, it's the business today," she was saying. "There are a lot of girls out there. You've got to compete. So I don't mind.

"The guys though, whew, they cover up with their hands. I mean, come on," she giggled, "like I was gonna look at that thing."

She shielded her crotch with long, delicate fingers that could have belonged to a pianist. But Edgar doubted that she had come from a home that would have ever been in a position to consider piano lessons.

"Why do you think that is?" Edgar asked her.

"'Cause it's all hanging out front," she

said simply. "Girls are more compact." She gave them a conspiratorial wink. "When the boys get a hard-on they really go nuts."

Edgar realized this talk coming from a male acquaintance would have seemed to him shocking. From Kelly, the waif, it was simply charming. She was two generations behind him and the world had changed and he had not changed with it. And while he was still uncomfortable with the language in movies, he realized those were the only movies Kelly knew.

"I only do art nudes," she said to Jake. "I wouldn't do anything else."

Edgar never doubted she was genuine. How many people bothered to think that the basis for most art and advertising was simply sexual?

"I only do art nudes."

She'd said it again—to reinforce her hopes? Her self-esteem? Maybe she was sensitive about doing nudes. But *Playhouse* magazine? How could she be? What made it art? Color photography?

Kelly didn't dress between takes. Gary offered her a robe. She said, "That's okay, I have my shirt," but she never put it on.

"Were you nervous in the beginning?" Edgar asked.

"Oh, yeah," Kelly said. "I was nervous the first time for about an hour. Then I was like, *ta tah*!" and she struck a pose with her arms wide apart.

She made him smile. He was not a guy noted for big smiles. Men with pipes in their mouths look very serious. Even after he stopped smoking the pipe, he looked like a pipe belonged in his mouth.

"Are you having fun yet?" he asked, trying to be one of the gang.

"Oh, yeah,"Kelly said from her position in the scene. "Time flies when you're having fun. Like sex," she said.

"I thought you had no social life," he said.

"What's the matter with doing it alone?" she said.

Edgar raised an eyebrow. Was she suggesting something? He was becoming uneasy.

"I'm gonna have me a hamburger when I get finished here," Kelly said. "I always pig out after a shoot."

"You don't look like a big eater."

"Oh, I eat like a pig."

"Really?" Edgar knew what a battle he had with the tire around his middle, "You eat ice cream?"

"Mmm, Häagen-Dazs. Love it. That no-fat stuff's a bunch of bullshit." She had an uncanny ability to stand stock still while she rattled on. The shadows had to hit her just so to cover the good stuff from the camera. Gary was fiddling with the light again.

"I'm going grocery shopping," she said. "I _love_ grocery shopping, it's the most fun. My roommate loves it when I go grocery shopping. I get her favorites, Snapple and bagels. It's like she has a wife. She was Treat of the Year. I was up for it but I didn't win."

"What did she get for that?"

"Two hundred and fifty thousand dollars."

"No!"

"Yes, she did. In cash and prizes."

"How much was cash?"

"She got something every month."

"How much?"

"Two or three thousand."

"For how long?"

"A year."

"Did she get a car?"

"She got a Cobra. But it was this puke green and she wanted to trade it for something more normal—and they were paying for it on time, you know, and they hadn't made all the payments or something. The whole thing was a real fuck-up—excuse my French."

Jake said something to Kelly that Edgar couldn't hear. It got her started on religion.

"My mother got all hepped up on religion while I was in high school. I was dumb—I didn't think anyone liked me. So I go to church with my mother and here's this preacher starting to talk like he knew everything about me—like God told him, he said, there was this girl with all these problems. Everybody knew it was me. I was humiliated. God didn't tell him nothin'—my mother told him. I never did forgive her that."

Jake said something else Edgar didn't hear.

"That's right," she said, "we can't show any puss in this."

Gary said he was ready, and with his automatic shutter blazing and one pause to reload the film, the session was over. Kelly hurried back to the chair, where she put on the tee shirt first, then the panties, making some dexterous adjust-

The Real Sleeper

ments as Edgar took one last, longing look. Then the shorts and corduroy shirt. Edgar may have imagined it, but he thought she took more pleasure taking off her clothes than putting them on.

"Do you like sushi?" Kelly asked Gary.

Gary said he loved sushi. So much for her hamburger talk. There wouldn't be any Häagen-Dazs for dessert, either.

Edgar didn't much like sushi, he thought, but he could learn.

But Kelly didn't invite him, and Gary claimed he was elsewhere engaged.

Kelly signed the release without reading it, and Edgar waited his turn to say goodbye to her.

Sushi, Edgar kept saying to himself. Tell her you like sushi and would love to go along.

But he couldn't get the words out. He thanked her again, and said, "You are very beautiful," but he got no sign that she had heard him.

Kelly stood dutifully still to receive the kiss he planted on her cheek. Just like his wife would stand: motionless. But Kelly's skin was so soft and smooth it was almost unreal to him.

Though the kiss could not have lasted more than a second, it seemed like Kelly waited patiently for him to desist. And then she was gone–out the door as briskly and suddenly as she had entered, leaving a surprising, empty ache in his chest.

After Kelly left, Jake brought in a brief-case from his car. "She's gone," he said, opening the case and showing Edgar the *Playhouse* magazine where Kelly was the Treat of the Month.

Edgar glanced at the pictures. And then, as they say in this generation, he lost it. He could see that these pictures were not such demure art nudes as advertised. Kelly was showing everything she had to show. A glance at Jake showed a leering, lecherous grin and Edgar exploded.

"God, it's disgusting men have to get their kicks from these poor girls posing like that."

"Hey, man," Jake said, lifting the magazine as though Edgar might engage in some disastrous censorship, "she posed for them. I didn't hold a gun at her head. All I did was buy the magazine."

He was right, of course, Edgar knew he should apologize for his outburst, but he couldn't. Kelly had become his responsibility and he had no idea if that would please her or annoy her. But no matter, it was just this stupid feeling

The Real Sleeper

that he never experienced before, and he didn't seem to be able to do anything about it.

The brochure Gary had sent him to get his approval of the model had her home phone written in the bottom-left corner.

What if he called her up and asked her out? Would she go to lunch with him—or laugh in his face?

On the way home, he stopped at a Hamburger Hamlet. Edgar had not eaten for seven hours, but he limited himself to a fruit shake and onion soup, deciding against the half-pound burger with the bacon and blue cheese dripping all over it, and the greasy fries he usually had. He needed to be in better shape.

Driving home, he passed a car with a girl about Kelly's age snuggled up to a driver and he wondered if that would ever happen to him.

How much time did he have left, after all? His grandparents had died in their fifties and sixties—his father just hit fifty-five before he went. Was it all genetically determined? he wondered.

It was time to sort out the important things.

KELLY

"He kissed me."

"Did you kiss him back?"

"Well, I did not. What do you think? I was just so shocked, I couldn't move. He must've thought I was some stick."

Me and my roommate, Bambi, were having our evening bagels at the Treat of the Year-prize table that served so many purposes in our loft apartment of one and a half floors. I was

The Real Sleeper

telling Bambi about my afternoon. Bambi's bed was on the main floor (she's the older by eleven months). I slept on the half floor, just up the ladder from Bambi's digs. Seniority wasn't the only factor in this division of floor space. Bambi paid more rent.

I always wondered if they could get a maid to live in one of those Holmby Hills mansions with a maid's room small as this. Especially now that it looked like a storage warehouse for a discount hard-goods store.

Bambi Barton, my roomie, was a blonde bombshell. I mean, she was a *real* knockout: long, flowing tresses, with a sun-bronzed body that got her to be *Playhouse* magazine's Treat of the Year, and all the windfall of merchandise that went with it.

Even though Bambi sounds like one of those made-up skin-mag names like Barbie, Bambi's mother named her that after the fawn in the movie of the same name. She was just nuts about that movie.

"During the shoot he was looking at me all the time," I said.

"At your body?" Bambi asked me.

"Well, yes."

"I get queasy when men leer."

"You wouldn't have them ignore you, would you?" I mean, come on. Sometimes Bambi was un*real*. "You don't take your clothes off so no one will look at you."

"But there's a difference in the looks. Frank sexuality is okay, I guess, but admiration is better."

"Yes, yes, and he had it," I said. "It was deeper—like a soul thing, a connecting of spirits of two entirely opposite people—you know, male and female and young and not so young, and all the rest of it. There's that special feeling that you can get over these basic differences and have this thing for each other."

"You felt that?" Bambi asked like she didn't believe me. "Really?"

"Yeah."

"Like, I mean, like a dad maybe?"

"No, not like a *dad*!" Sometimes Bambi was so dense. "Like a, you know, a real considerate lover."

"Oh, wow!"

Me and Bambi had to move the dining table out into the room to get the two chairs around it.

The Real Sleeper

Nothing in the place matched anything else. The mess of Bambi's different prizes just took over our pad.

The plastic kayak was standing on edge in the corner of the main floor. Against the longest wall was the entertainment center wall unit of darkish walnut. It held the stereo, but not the speakers—they didn't fit on the shelves and stood on both sides of the wall unit. They were crafted of beechwood and contained an eight-inch woofer, five-inch midrange, plus tweeter for clear transparent highs extended to beyond 40kHz.

The large-screen television set in dynamic modern black didn't fit on the wall unit either. It was on the floor in front of the card table and four chairs, which, since we were so short of space, were folded behind the TV.

On the shelf, the ultimate in turntable design, including the premier studio tone arm, in case you had any phonograph records (we didn't). This unit was of blonde wood and hung out over the shelf some four inches. Also on the shelf, the voiceprint voice-dialing telephone, the motorcycle helmet and the 1.4x teleconverter, 40468 0.8x wide-angle converter, 28932 GS 320 flash, 2761Z deluxe neck strap, 2754S hold-all case, 28866 lithium battery, and 985150 AA battery (4).

In the center of the room (we didn't have a garage), courtesy of the Suzuki Corporation, the red, white and blue GS 500E motorcycle kinda took over. I mean, the GS 500E so took over the room that me and Bambi had to mount the seat and swing our legs over it to get from the kitchen to the ladder going up to my loft, or to Bambi's bed (a convertible couch) and back again.

Upstairs, in my part of the loft, were the matched set of luggage (five pieces), the fish-aquarium floor-model clock (empty), the state-of-the-art collapsible London Shade (collapsed and folded under the bed, but sticking out two feet at the foot). The black mountain bike was between the bed and the wall, making pedestrian passage on that side of the bed inadvisable.

At the foot of the bed, straddling the London Shade, the TV-1450, AD-K64 (adaptor), CT-656, and CS-20 (stand) from Casio, Inc. (That's a portable keyboard.)

We had talked about moving up to a bigger place, but we realized the extra two grand cash per month our Treat of the Year won was good for only a year, and then we knew we would have to move down again. And we probably wouldn't find such a cool place like this for the price.

That pile of bagels on the prize table between us girls was sure going down. I couldn't believe we ate so much.

Bambi had on an open-necked white blouse over her jeans, and in that open neck hung the gold medallion that proclaimed her Treat of the Year, with ruby-studded crowns and scepters.

Bambi won that one and I didn't. We didn't compete in the same year or anything, so I wasn't that bummed out. Besides, I was a brunette and blondes always won. Besides, Bambi was so nice, she never lorded it over me or anything. And she let me share all the prizes. I mean, like if I wanted to take the motorcycle out for a spin, it was cool with her. Of course, I wouldn't do such a thing. I mean, what if something happened to it?

The only thing she wouldn't share was that ruby-studded medallion around her neck. That was strictly and exclusively for the Treat of the Year.

Kelly

I always did wonder how they picked one girl over another for that honor. I mean, you knew it was going to a blonde, but heck, there were a lot of blondes. Maybe it was politics with the photographers or something. Naturally you had to have big tits, and Bambi had *those* all right. Or it could have been how much puss you showed. And there wasn't anybody beat out Bambi in that category.

"He was a lamb, Bambi," I was saying, "I swear. You could just cuddle him."

"Oh, Kelly. How old is he?"

"Oh, I don't know exactly. Old, for sure. At least forty-five."

"Hm. Looking for a sugar daddy?"

"What's wrong with that?"

"There's worse things, I guess."

"There isn't much happening to us as it is."

Bambi got that sad, frowny look on her face, she did when you said something she didn't want to hear. I knew she didn't like that "reality talk," she called it. We'd had many discussions before about our predicament. Pretty faces and, yes, gorgeous tits and ass were a dime a dozen in this town. And, sure, both of us could get guys all we want for sex, but after a while you get to wonder if there isn't more to it.

Did we spoil our chances showing too much? Did we get a bad reputation that smelled like a skunk?

Until things got better, we went to bed at seven o'clock.

"He smiled at me." I was getting kind of dreamy at the memory.

"Does he have a sports car?" Bambi was being practical.

"Gosh, I don't know. He doesn't seem like the type though."

"But you got a crush on him anyways?"

"Now, I didn't say that. But he *is* a man and you know I favor men, and these days a straight man is worth his weight in gold."

"How is his weight?"

"Well, *Bambi*! Why do you ask such a thing?"

"He is older, isn't he? Most of 'em have big guts."

"I guess he does," I admitted, remembering him in his suit. "I told him that fat-free diet stuff was a bunch of bullshit. You think I was wrong?"

Kelly

"I hear when you get older it's not so much bullshit as when you're twenty. Sticks to your ribs a little better. Metabolism and all."

"Yeah. Well, he's cute anyway," I said. "Looks like the daddy you wished you had."

"Or granddaddy?" Bambi scoffed.

"Well, okay, yeah, maybe. Either way..."

EDGAR

Driving home from the photo session, on 101 North to Thousand Oaks, I noticed the bright sunshine and reveled in it. On the way down, I hadn't noticed it at all.

The drive from the freeway to our house in Thousand Oaks was always pleasant. The streets reeled with towering willowy things that made me feel small. I never knew the names of them, botany was not a field that ever caught my fancy.

Our street was newer than the main artery, so the trees were not as tall.

I couldn't think of our home without an acute sense of irony. Here we were, Penelope and I, two born-and-bred Easterners living in this anachronous Spanishy pastiche which doesn't exist where we came from. Everyone got to land-scape their own property, giving the houses a semblance of originality, yet it was surprising how many of them wound up with a grass lawn and specimen olive tree.

When the East Coast Wellingtons arrived on the West Coast, the cost of housing was out of sight in Los Angeles County, for a one-teacher-income family. But the further you went from the heart of things, the more affordable houses became, assuming you were willing to stretch the word "affordable" to its critical limits.

As it turned out, the house we bought was more or less in between our livelihoods. A little closer to Penelope's perhaps, but she had the larger income.

I parked my Ford Escort in the garage. My heart gave a little skip when I noticed

The Real Sleeper

Penelope's Lincoln Town Car was not in its place.

After I found Penelope's note about going to Atlanta, I went right to the empty bedroom I used for a studio and got out my paints and brushes.

Our house was a three bedroom. The first floor had a two-story living room, the balance of the living areas and the master suite. Upstairs had the two remaining bedrooms and a shared bath. It's a big place for two people; a couple kids would have filled it up nicely.

The house decor reflected Penelope's taste: austere. I didn't care much about decor. I hung my favorite paintings in my studio, but my art didn't appear anywhere else in the house.

I don't make waves.

I don't know why, exactly, I drew and painted Kelly O'Leary in such heat. Maybe it was to get her out of my system—to forget this impossible dream of mine once and for all. If that *was* the reason, it didn't succeed. The more I painted her, the more I wanted her.

The house was empty and quiet, the way I like it. Penelope spends most of her time at home on the phone, stirring the pot of academic politics, which, in my limited experience, will boil over whether you stir it or not.

We have our own phone lines, but I rarely use mine. It has atrophied into a hot line for my eighty-five-year-old mother. She is my hope for longevity, being the family's stubborn holdout against premature transmogrification to fertilizer.

With the doors closed on cold days, I didn't hear much of Penelope's conversations, but on the warmer days we liked to keep the doors open and it was sometimes annoying, her incessant chatter and hefty laughter.

I married Penelope because she took the operation and administration of the courtship into her capable hands. I don't know what she wanted with me except possibly that it was *de rigueur* to have a husband and, if nothing else, I looked like an academic. And, I was tall enough for her; we're both on the brink of six feet.

I didn't ask her for any free samples before the pagan ceremony because I thought it a tacky imposition on chaste womanhood. Besides, I was afraid she would get pregnant and bury us all in scandal. And, of course, I was afraid to ask.

I was, simply, repressed.

Commencing with the marriage ritual, our roles reversed. I sought libidinous fulfillment, but she evidenced no interest.

It seemed almost immediate that she decided "all that sloppy business with the mouths" was unappetizing. If you ever tried to kiss a closed refrigerator door, you will have an idea about how much pleasure I got trying to kiss her. But, I never blamed her. I guess I didn't have the virility for it. I thought instead that we are what we are, and though you can fight it, you can hardly change it.

We have no kids—not for the obvious reasons, but simply because Penelope didn't want them. She said she wouldn't mind having them, she just didn't want to take care of them.

When I called her bluff and said I would take care of them, she changed her tune to a flat out "No kids, asshole!"

She calls me that from time to time when she is especially angry. I have told her I don't like it, but she claims she can't help it. Though I suspect she was able to "help it" at the university, where the provocations were at least as great.

Edgar

Sure, I've considered divorce. Who hasn't? On the surface, in California, nothing could be easier. "Irreconcilable differences" is all you need claim. Everyone has irreconcilable differences. Those who stay married reconcile them.

It always seemed to me you had to be rich to get divorced. Look at us: two educated, fairly well-employed people who could barely make it in Southern California on their own. The house would be the first to go. I had a friend who spent eighty thousand on lawyers' fees, about half his net worth. His wife got less than the lawyers.

So we compromised. Maybe we never did reconcile those differences, but we sublimated them. Perhaps it was not only the house but our own sense of propriety that kept us together.

Lately, I'd begun to question the value of that "propriety." How, I wondered, would my life have been different if I had married someone less intellectual than Penelope—more earthy, like Kelly?

Perhaps deep down, all women are disinterested. Penelope may just be more honest about it. Or maybe I just didn't have the spark necessary to ignite any fires in her.

The Penelope and Edgar Wellington story was not a page turner. I loved books, so I thought I should teach literature. But, I had no talent for teaching. I wasn't a salesman. I couldn't sell my love of books to my students, just as I couldn't sell my love to my wife.

Penelope was always the star of the zoology faculty, wherever she taught. (I was teaching at Rutgers, she ended her East Coast stint at Princeton.) Then the inevitable happened: she got an offer neither of us could refuse. It was for more money than we were both earning. It was so exciting for her, we never questioned the bulbous prices for housing in the Los Angeles area.

Penelope settled in as a department head at USC and I settled in being unemployed. I guess my (lack of) zest for teaching literature was obvious, so I finally got a job an hour from home in the opposite direction from Penelope's work. A rich dilettante who made his money making missile gaskets decided to redeem himself to society by pouring his ill-gotten gains into publishing fine books. He liked my academic credentials and hired me. The books haven't all been that fine, but it's an undemanding living and I can't complain.

Exhausted by my immersion in the sensuality and smells of oil paint and brushes, I began drawing pencil-line pictures of Kelly, erasing the lines, then redrawing them.

As I filled in the outlines of Kelly's delicate face, I visualized her nude and heard again her gentle protestation, "I only do art nudes." I couldn't fault her for it. Who among us does not harbor outrageous conceits about our livelihoods? "We only publish important books at Oak Tree Press." "I only taught worthy literature in my classes."

"Shall I get nude?" I heard her say over and over again in my mind. Then I saw her dance to the chair to take off her androgynous outer garments and her feminine panties. The simple joy she seemed to have doing that, I tried so hard to capture in my painting. But thinking about her youth and beauty forced me to think about my approaching milestone birthday and the great gap between us.

I suppose it is inevitable as we age we turn to thoughts of the end. It is a cliché that "old" people read the obituaries first, not only to see if someone they know was less fortunate ("It is not enough to succeed, a friend must fail."— La Rochefoucauld) but to see how long the strangers lasted.

Of course, I don't know many people of obituary magnitude, but I do take a cursory glance to kind of figure the averages. But, I see this deathwatch other places too.

We take a closer look at old parties in public. Some old guy being helped from his chair at a restaurant table—gray in pallor, hunched over, walking only with the assist of two healthy males. If you had the choice, would you want to last long enough to be helpless? I try not to think about it. In the meantime I am checking the averages in the obits.

The toughest thing for me is visiting my mother in the old-folks' home. A joyless place, a holding tank for the Grim Reaper. What quality is there left in these sedated lives? We have drugs for everything now. The oldsters walk around the halls (those who can still walk) like zombies. They've taken their oral lobotomies and they are less of a nuisance because of it.

I fell asleep at my easel. I had forgotten to eat. When I awoke an hour and a half later, I thought I should drag myself to bed.

Instead, I rummaged around and found my stash of *Playhouse* magazines and ordered the back issue wherein Kelly O'Leary was Treat of the Month. Then I ordered the ski machine they had advertised.

Then I dropped to the floor and accomplished four half-baked, but painful, sit-ups.

Tomorrow I would do six.

PENELOPE

Not too flattering, is it? Edgar's view of me, I mean. Like kissing a closed refrigerator door! He never discusses this with me, he's so introverted and circumspect. Mealy-mouthed, you might call it. You wonder how you could be married to someone for thirty-five years and not know anything about them. He apparently knows nothing at all about me.

He says he couldn't get me to read his

manuscripts. Well, is it any wonder? Look at the pretentious words he uses: "premature *transmogrification* to fertilizer"? Really! I stopped reading because I couldn't praise him. He stood around like a dog who had just retrieved a bird, his tail wagging for dear life, and I couldn't rub him behind the ears. I just couldn't fake it. Being honest has its advantages, but it has its drawbacks too.

Edgar talks about his mother, and father the Doc. He had it good. My parents divorced when I was eleven—and it was nothing but fights before that. I used to escape to my room, where I read books and vowed never to get married.

I figure I came close to keeping that vow. Being married to Edgar is as close as you can come to being unmarried.

We live like roommates, passing in the hall. I talk and he doesn't listen.

Okay, I don't listen much either, but Edgar doesn't say much. I've gotten more insight reading this stuff he's written than I have in a lifetime of living with him.

I don't remember anyone hugging me as a child. I think my mother thought those signs of affection déclassé. I suppose, as a result, I'm not very huggy. Actually, the only times I remember being held by my mother were when I was vomiting in the toilet. Edgar has shunned doing that for me.

Okay, Edgar may not understand me, but he certainly knows more about me than he is letting on. I frankly think it is a little sneaky writing those things about me. Not to say unfair and misleading.

He sounds so meek and helpless. He's not. I have been the major breadwinner, but that is not by choice. I would gladly have stepped aside anytime had Edgar shown the slightest gumption about supporting us.

As we girls get older the heart flutters slower and less often. It's supposed to be that way with the men too—*cf.* Edgar's dad's poem. Edgar seems bent on reversing nature. Well, more power to him. After he achieves that he can try his hand at milking butterflies.

First of all, he's no Mel Gibson. And I don't care what they say about love handles and more to love, I don't find overweight men seductive.

I am especially interested to see Edgar's opinions on my sensuality. I always wonder what his standard is. He admits he has no other experience.

Before we were married, I offered him the store, but no, he didn't want any "scandal." Imagine! If he had been more adventuresome he could have found me wanting and nipped the engagement in the bud.

Of course, I realized too late it was all a mistake. But by then the invitations were out, the dress was bought, the caterer had his deposit. And then the gifts began to come in. Nobody wants to look like a fool, so I relaxed and enjoyed it as much as I could, realizing I had made a major faux pas with my life.

Just as an indication of how far around the bend Edgar has gone, he's cut out of the *New Yorker* this ad for sensual products:

> **We guarantee that the product you choose will keep giving you pleasure.** Should it malfunction, simply return it to us for a replacement.

Ha! What if *he* malfunctions?

I do hope you have noticed how repulsive he finds my occasional expletives and how charming he finds the same from Bimbo.

All this reading of his notes makes me think of the Tolstoys exchanging their diaries. And brutally frank they were. Maybe I should show Edgar my thoughts. I'm just not sure he could take it in the state he's in. Maybe when he gets over the bimbo we can both have a good laugh about it.

I never thought I'd live to see Edgar pumping iron. But there he is, grunting and groaning, the barbells thumping on the floor after some quasi-successful lift.

His room is starting to look like a gymnasium with all the equipment he's bought. He's got the ski machine, the barbells, and he's even just strung up a punching bag. I guess that is preferable to using me for the same purpose.

I can hardly resist sneaking a peek at him when he is huffing and puffing, struggling to keep his feet in the ski-machine stirrups, manfully trying to lift those barbells one more time. I have to give him this, however, he is starting to look better. It is simply a crime that men can lose weight so much more easily than women.

I've taken a vicarious interest in the numerous drafts (more accurately *over*drafts) of what I call *My Life with Bimbo*.

I know her type: low intellectual capacity, minimal education, one of those girls who chewed gum surreptitiously in the back of her biology class, who wore tight short skirts, working her *ass*et for all it was worth.

They had bodies we thought would never stop. But everything stops—I should know.

A thought just occurred to me: Edgar could be leaving these writings around to mislead me. Maybe he *has* gotten further with Bimbo than he says. But that's not Edgar. He hasn't got a deceptive bone in his body.

At least he didn't used to have.

EDGAR

What to say on the telephone to a twenty-three-year-old model who I had watched nude for almost two hours did not come easily. What would she think if I called her? A dirty old man?

Sunday morning I usually devote to reading the *New York Times*. It shoots two and a half, three hours. I wondered if ever in her life Kelly has even seen the *New York Times*.

And there in the opinion section they had

a story on sex. They'd done a survey about sexual practices. What do you do? How often do you do it? How many partners last year, how many partners total—how old are you?

And then it grabbed me. I had been reading these sophisticated breakdowns until I got to the last group and looked for more. Ages fifty-five to fifty-nine were the end. They didn't bother with anyone older than fifty-nine. Presumably they would be too old to produce statistics.

Where do they find these people, men yet, who only think of sex a few times a month? No one over fifty-nine in this survey, remember. They weren't asking octogenarians zonked out on tranquilizers in nursing homes. These are the red bloods. But who? Some truck driver doesn't think about it—a policeman—a judge?

A lot has happened over the last week. First I got the transparencies from Gary, the photographer for the book cover. He sent twenty-four of them—half of what he'd taken. He took them so fast they are practically identical and none of the shadows really cover the parts of Kelly which must be covered if we are to have any hope of getting the books in the stores and libraries.

I called Gary and he assured me the lab

could easily cover whatever I wanted.

Looking at these transparencies again and again in order to select the "best" one made me want to be with Kelly more than ever. But, the more I wanted her, the more afraid I was to talk to her. I don't think it was rejection I feared—I'd had enough of that to build a nice, protective immunity. Rather, I think, I was afraid to upset her, insult her, make her uncomfortable.

This week I gave the punching bag, barbells, and ski machine a real workout.

My efforts at losing weight were amply rewarded. I could button my pants without the waistband cutting into my flesh, and button my shirts without the parenthesis appearing between the buttons. Before you know it I will have removed one more obstacle in the path of asking Kelly to lunch.

Toward the end of that week, I got the *Playhouse* magazine—in the plain wrapper, cellophane-sealed against innocent eyes.

I tore into it like a starving kid tears into a candy bar.

The magazine opened to Kelly. She was at one with the staples in the center of the pages. I thought sheepishly of my accidental anger at the male model, whose name and face I had already forgotten. It was as though, because of my tantrum, I had no right to look at these pictures.

Looking at Kelly's body now, I saw how much more of it she was showing. There weren't any girl-next-door poses like there were in her brochure. In every one of the twenty-one pictures she was sporting a sultry look. But it didn't seem to belong to her. Kelly in person was adorable. She was pert, alive, candid and down-home. Anything but sultry. Maybe that was the schtick for the month.

I checked the pictures of the other girls. Pretty much sultry. There were a few dreamy looks on one of the blondes, but brunettes like Kelly are doomed to be sultry.

I don't know how much time I spent gazing and fantasizing. And how many men would do the same? Young, good-looking, in-shape guys. They sold millions of these magazines. I closed *Playhouse* and stared out of my studio window. What chance did I have with Kelly O'Leary? Slim to none.

I couldn't reach for the phone.

A couple days later, I sat at my desk at work, amid the walls of books, Kelly's pictures and the galleys of the book she was going to be on. I realized I didn't want to lose that magic of hers. Slowly, I got up and closed my office door. Then I returned to my desk in something of a trance. Without any conscious thought, I dialed Kelly's number, which I had memorized.

She picked it up on the second ring.

"Hello?"

"Hi. Is this the incomparable Kelly O'Leary?"

"Who's this?"

"It's Edgar Wellington—from the book-cover shoot."

"Oh, how are you?"

"Fine, how are you?"

"Fine."

There was a pause while I groped for something else to say. I was busy chastising myself for not planning this better. I was not a guy who did *anything* on impulse, let alone anything as important as this was, and now I was paying the price of my impetuosity.

"Well," she said finally, "it's nice of you to call. How've you been?"

"Fine," I said, thinking the question had a familiar cast to it.

"How about you?" I asked.

"Just fine."

"That's good."

There was another devastating lull in the conversational intercourse, which Kelly, being the cooler head, was the first to break.

"Well, geez, guy, thanks for calling. I got to run to an interview now, but I hope you'll call again, hear?"

"I will," I muttered, before I hung up, dispirited.

This is crazy, I told myself. Almost sixty years old and fumbling around trying to date a twenty-year-old—just who is the twelve-year-old in this equation?

I sank back in my chair, my lungs heaving with the excitement of it all.

Then I thought of how wonderfully sweet she'd sounded.

KELLY

"Oh, man," I groaned when I hung up the voice-activated phone, and replaced it on Bambi's bookshelf. "He must think I'm the biggest dork!"

"Who?" Bambi asked.

"That was Edgar." I threw my leg over the motorcycle seat.

"Who's Edgar?" Bambi asked from the

dinette table and chairs.

"You *know*, the guy from the book-cover shoot."

"Oh, Grandpa."

"Bambi!" Sometimes she got me so mad I could scream. "I mean, I could hardly *speak*, I was so riled up. I mean, I made up a story—I lied to him because I was too nervous to think of anything to say."

"That's a novelty," Bambi said.

"He must just think I'm the biggest dork."

"Oh, I don't know," Bambi said, eying me with her cool, superior look, "I've seen bigger."

PENELOPE

I didn't mean to confess this, but I have this stupid guilt feeling about it. This morning, before Edgar was awake, I went into his room to read what he had written about me last night after he got back out of bed. I knew what he was going to say and I thought it rather unfair, so I just took the offending pages from the manuscript. I tore them in little pieces and put them down the garbage disposal. I realize that may seem like overkill, but that's just the way I felt about it at the time. I'm sure he intended for that nasty interlude to place the blame on me for his finally getting the nerve to call the bimbo. So I nipped it in the bud.

The way Edgar writes it you'd think I was a sexless shrew who rejects Mr. Prince Charming all the time. He can't seem to ever get it through his head that when I don't feel like it I'm not going to do it. This "Oh, sweetie, not tonight please—okay, snookums?" stuff is not in my nature.

He says, "Change your nature," but I don't see him changing his. It will be interesting to see if Edgar misses it. It was only two pages and I really think that when he cooled down and reread it he would have taken it out himself to spare my feelings. Edgar isn't a cruel man. That's not in *his* nature.

All the same, I wasn't taking any chances.

Of course, if he does reread what he wrote and misses it, he will know what happened. Then he will confront me. He might even be pleased that I am reading his stuff.

He wants this, he wants that, but people are not alone in this world. When what you want involves the cooperation of someone else, you may not always get it.

All right, I admit it. I was in his room again. Looking for the map book he keeps there. There I saw all these wild pictures he is drawing and painting. Even if I was a psychiatrist, I'm not sure I could make sense of what he's done.

He has drawing after drawing of this bimbo's head and body parts. There is a big canvas started which apparently is going to depict her breasts south to the pubic region. Another shows a rear view. All buns.

I always thought Edgar too obsessed with sex, but I have never seen such graphic evidence of it.

Edgar, you should know, is not much of a painter. I don't see any harm in it, but we won't have to worry about tax problems from his painting.

I honestly don't know which is worse, Edgar's writing or his painting. There isn't an ounce of objectivity or self-censorship in either.

But now, he's making me curious. He's got this *Playhouse* magazine hidden under a pile of his sketches. It has the bimbo he's painting, and she's showing it all, believe me. God, men like it raw, don't they? Poor Edgar, to have to resort to pictures.

I leafed through this smutty skin magazine and good God, listen to this. From the Treat of the Year:

"Acting as an ambassador and spokesperson for *Playhouse* is even a greater honor than being Miss America...men will view me as a symbol of quality, class and respectability—and hopefully, women will agree."

My God in heaven! Class and respectability? From exposing your genitals?

As I paged through this stupid magazine I thought, if you've seen one, you've seen them all. Then I noticed that was not so. There were variations in those gynecological folds and in the color, shape, thickness and density of the hair.

I suppose it could have the same bizarre appeal as, say, collecting fountain pens does for some people. All the pens do the same thing and are shaped basically alike, but the joy is in the infinite variety of those functional objects: the nuances of design and the subtly differing approaches to the same function.

Being a zoologist, I tend to look at the big picture—five billion of us trying to be important, trying to be well-thought-of. That's what it's all about. From the streets to the cocktail circuit, there is posturing and pretension.

But isn't trying to be well-thought-of the root of this boy/girl thing? Very few of us can be famous (I won't go into the destruction wrought by fame). So if you succeed with one member of the opposite (not to say opposing) sex, you have achieved being well-thought-of in the eyes of at least one person.

Did Edgar ever think well of me? I suppose. Though I don't credit his carnality with any perceived worth on my part. Sometimes I think sheep and chickens would do him.

But did I ever think well of him? I honestly can't remember, though I must have.

As for rejecting him—having no passion—after a day at the plant and an hour-plus ride home I'm strung out. I *am* the major breadwinner after all and some allowance should be made for that. If the major breadwinner is a man, you bet *major* allowances are made.

Though I doubt Edgar would ever credit me, I have made some considerable efforts in his behalf.

I asked my gynecologist for a hormone

treatment, but when he told me that there were horrendous side effects, I just decided I didn't want hair crawling all over my face and body. I _do_ have a job after all; I can't go around looking like an orangutan.

So instead, Edgar's got these magazines with Bimbo bent over a pile of her pink underwear, or she's on a boat with one knee here and the other one in Texas.

Men are nuts. I'll never understand them. You'd think with a Ph.D. in zoology I'd have a leg up with the species. _Some_ species perhaps, but I doubt there is anyone, Ph.D. or no, who can understand _this_ two-legged species.

I think I'll go crazy if I have to listen to one more Ella Fitzgerald rendition of "Bewitched, Bothered and Bewildered." Edgar plays it over and over like a moonstruck adolescent. I never was too taken with alliteration anyway.

> I'm wild again,
> Beguiled again,
> A simpering,
> Whimpering
> Child again—

A-men, brother. Larry Hart could write lyrics, but Frank Lloyd Wright could design houses too, and we'd get mighty tired of a whole hillside full of the same house.

Well, let him go, I say. I've told him from the beginning he could have his fling. Sex is nothing to get hysterical about. It's just a fact of life like birth and death. No big deal.

No, I'm not worried about diseases. For Edgar to contract a disease, he would have to *do* something.

And I know Edgar better than that.

Edgar is happiest alone, wrapped around some book or painting his childish pictures. To have an affair, you have to *speak* to someone. That's not Edgar.

I'm not worried.

EDGAR

I don't know when it was that I finally got around to reading the words on Kelly's *Playhouse* spread. But I'll never forget the one line that jumped out at me: "The man who gives me the keys to his sports car wins my heart forever."

I didn't have a sports car. But that didn't mean I couldn't get one.

I had always ranked shopping for a car as the low point in my life. The rank deception, outright lying and sleazy practices I came to associate with buying a car always got me down.

Today was different. I didn't feel any pressure. I didn't fear being flummoxed. I couldn't even think of the salesmen and their nefarious tricks to make you think you are paying one price while jacking it up elsewhere under the guise of prorated advertising—an invisible laser number in the windshield. I was having fun.

Of course, I knew nothing about cars, less about sports cars. I had to ask what set a sports car apart from a sporty small car. The answers I got were not always satisfying, logical or even reasonable, but they were always amusing.

"Horsepower? What's the cutoff?"

"Well, it's not that simple—"

"Price?"

"Not really…"

"What's the demarcation line?"

"Not that simple—"

"The lines of the car—low to the ground?"

I would point out a small car that looked sporty to me, but no dice.

I could tell a lot of the salesmen put me in what they called their "Looky-Loo" category.

Some could barely bring themselves to answer my questions. Others were dubious about an old jerk who looked so staid and stolid, but were too hungry to run the risk of losing a sale, no matter how remote the possibility seemed.

No one offered me a test drive (what if a live one came in while they were out on the road with the old jerk?).

"Ready to buy a car today?" one earnest middle-aged chap with black, curly hair slicked down with something that smelled like axle grease, asked me.

"Oh, I don't know. I'm shopping."

"Well, why don't you come back when you've made up your mind?"

"Without driving the car? Do people do that? Buy a car without driving it?" Then I giggled.

"What's so funny?"

"Oh, nothing," I said. It seemed to put him off his feed. I was thinking of Penelope saying you wouldn't buy a pair of shoes without trying them on, in reference to intimacy before marriage. Here I was shopping for an intimacy incentive.

I finally found a salesman willing to "take

her out for a spin," as he put it. For a moment, I thought he was referring to Kelly as "her," and not the little, low-slung, red convertible job on the showroom floor.

All the preparations were made, my license was photocopied. Temporary plates were brought out and hung over the bumper. The salesman said for "insurance purposes" he had to put the car on the street. I think that they thought I would get hit or hit something on the way out of the lot, so he drove me to some quiet back road, where he turned the wheel over to me.

It was sort of fun. I tried to visualize how Kelly would look behind the wheel. How her smile would burgeon. I tried to feel as she would feel: exhilarated. But I couldn't. I kept wondering what the salesman thought: of me, my driving, and if he had any chance in the world of a sale.

He gave me what must have been the standard pitch about the beauty of the machinery: "Feel those horses, what incredible power. It's so responsive — go ahead, slam on the brakes — safety with a capital S."

I was grateful he treated me like a "live one." Though I could tell he was very much afraid I was close to being a dead one.

Edgar

Naturally, I drove the car onto the lot. Perhaps while we were out for the spin the car dealership signed with a more liberal insurance company.

When they talked price and terms, I turned shy. Maybe I should get to know her first, I thought. What if I just drove up to Kelly's apartment and handed her the keys and she laughed in my face? What would I do with a sports car then? *I* didn't want a sports car.

✻   ✻   ✻

I got the package with the book and cover off to the printer. It made me feel a great sense of loss. I still had my transparencies, and I still had my *Playhouse* magazine with Kelly as the Treat of the Month, but I still felt funny.

Perhaps it was because I had set in motion the climax of the relationship. I had promised myself that when the book was finished and the covers were back I would take the book to Kelly personally.

I knew it would be about six weeks before

the books came, and in that time my fantasy could dissipate. It had happened before. But I had never been this close to the object before. Never felt quite as intensely involved. This time my fantasy was alive and well, but should I really chance another six weeks?

No, damn it, I thought, I'm not waiting. I'm asking her to lunch. Maybe that'll kill it. She seemed encouraging when I called before, but maybe she's got a boyfriend by now. One closer to her age. Maybe she won't go out with me— even to lunch. Maybe if I sat down with her alone I'd be put off by her limited education.

There were so many things to think about. Should I lie about my age? Should I try to make myself seem younger without actually lying? What should I say about my marriage—if she brought it up? I wouldn't bring it up, of course, but better be prepared, just in case.

This time I wasn't going to make a fool of myself telephoning. I made a neat list of things to say, and then, being the good editor, I went back over the list and made alterations.

I looked down at the final list on my desk in my Santa Barbara office—for any last-minute additions or corrections.

1. Sent book and cover.
2. You looked sensational.
3. What have you been doing?
4. Any good jobs?
5. Got the *Playhouse* with you in it. You look smashing.
6. Is it true what it says in there, that you like to be admired? *I* admire you.
7. And you'd give your heart to the man who gave you the keys to his sports car?
8. I went sports car shopping.
9. What kinds do you like?
10. Would you have lunch with me sometime—or dinner?

I looked up from the list and out the window at a sparkling day—the bright spring sunshine bouncing off the delicate leaves of the ancient tree in the front of the old Victorian that housed the Oak Tree Press. And it wasn't an oak tree out front, but a Christmassy-looking thing. Suddenly the sun was in full retreat and a blanket of clouds threw a pall over that old tree.

I looked at the phone on my desk—friend or foe?

The Real Sleeper

    I hesitated. I dithered. I told myself I didn't fear rejection, I feared making her feel uncomfortable—a married guy asking her out. She'd probably think I only wanted one thing. Was that inaccurate?

    Come on now, I chided myself—you're just procrastinating—like they say in that shoe ad, just *do* it.

KELLY

"Wheeee! Bambi! He called again. We're going *out*!"

"Who, that old guy?"

"Bambi! He is *so* nice. I can't wait for you to meet him." I was so excited, I could hardly see straight. We were sitting at the prize dinette table where we usually sat when there was nothing doing. It was really the only place we could sit together since Bambi won all the prizes for being

Treat of the Year. It was kind of a crummy day outside, but I was just feeling like the sun was shining away.

"When's he coming?" Bambi asked.

"Saturday night. He's getting us reservations at Pierre Francois—isn't that exciting?"

"Wow!" Bambi flapped her hand, "Uptown."

"I *guess!*"

"Is he bringing his wife with him?"

"Well, no, he is not," I said. "What kind of a question is that?" Sometimes Bambi can be just the wettest blanket.

"Catty," Bambi admitted. "Sorry."

"You'll like him, Bam, I just know you will." All of a sudden I noticed I was biting my thumb cuticle. It was a habit I'd been trying for-*ever* to break. "Are you going to be here Saturday?"

"Far's I know," Bambi said. "Now, Kelly O'Leary—you can't be so anxious about these things. You don't want him to think you are too easy."

"But I *am* easy," I said. I thought she *knew* that.

"But that's no way to catch a man. You

got to be a little hard to get."

"Ha! That's real good advice coming from the girl who picked up that gorgeous George fella and came back home while I was in the loft. I never heard such a goings on!"

"I had too much to drink," Bambi explained. "He was just a roll in the hay, I'd a never done that if I was trying to impress him."

Bambi was so good at justifying her actions. "Well, I guess I'll just have to play it by ear."

"Don't mind me," Bambi said. "You do what you think is best. I'll arrange with Sheri if you want."

"Well, I don't know yet what I'll do," I said. "Maybe if I come back here with him, we can have some kind of signal. I can say something like, oh, I don't know, how about if I say, 'Edgar, would you like to buy a motorcycle?' And if I say that, you say, 'Nice to meet you, I gotta run—I told Sheri I'd be over,' or something. Oh, Bambi, I'm just so excited. He's just the *nicest* man."

"Good," Bambi got a little softer, "I'm so happy for you."

"Guess what?" I said.

"What?"

"He went shopping for a sports car, because he read in *Playhouse* where I said I'd give my heart to the man who gave me the keys to his sports car. Isn't that dear?"

"That *is*!" Bambi said, and she worked up some enthusiasm to go along with it—before she asked the inevitable damper: "Did he buy it?"

"Well, no, he did not buy it, what do you think? He said he decided he'd better see if I would go out with him first. Isn't that just the sweetest thing?"

"It's the *sweetest*!" Bambi cooed and looked like she did when she was playing the martyr. But she couldn't throw an old dishrag at my spirits. I was so excited about seeing Edgar, it's like I peed in my pants.

EDGAR AND KELLY

Kelly had said dinner would be safer because she never knew when she would have an interview or a shoot in the daytime.

Edgar invited Kelly for the Saturday night Penelope was going to be in Denver for some conference or other on some zoological phenomenon or other—he couldn't keep track.

He had worked like a mad fiend on the ski machine in excited anticipation of his "date."

Every time he got rational about the thing, he came close to talking himself out of it. But then he told himself he had been rational all his life and what did he have to show for it?

Edgar knocked off a bunch more pounds and by the appointed Saturday he had broken two hundred—for the first time in more than ten years.

He took an eon in the shower, scrubbing himself so hard it was a miracle there was any skin left. Secretly he hoped the excessive motions would tear off some more fat. He washed and conditioned his hair, then when he finally ran out of hot water and was forced out of the shower, he brushed his teeth for the third time in as many hours.

He had allowed plenty of time for the trip to Kelly's place, just in case he got stuck in traffic. She seemed so excited about his choice of restaurants he didn't want to disappoint her by being too late for the table.

He had made another list of things to say to her, so he wouldn't come off as a complete nerd. When he was finally dressed, he checked his pocket to make sure he had the list.

He wore his severest suit of dark navy with

a sporty denim shirt and red-and-blue-splotched tie. He preferred the old preppie Ivy League look, but he was taking out a girl from the new generation, after all; and when in *Roma*...

Kelly lived around the corner from the commerce on Santa Monica Boulevard. It was a faded greenish stucco building of two to three irregular stories. Edgar got a parking spot only a half block up the street. He parked, checked himself in the rearview mirror, primped his hair a bit, straightened his tie, then got out of the car and put on his jacket. Edgar never wore his jacket in the car. It mussed it.

So much of the town was stucco, he thought. And so much of that stucco had faded pastel paint. The newer buildings seemed to favor earthy beige tones. You could usually tell a place that was pretty old by its color.

And the postwar building boom saw a lot of minimal construction in multiple dwellings, of which this was one. Linguini-thin fascia boards and no decorative add-ons to the walls of unrelieved stucco. They went up fast and they went up cheap, these war babies. Edgar climbed the Diato stairs. A material called magnesite made these lightweight concrete stairs which always cracked, and cracked these were. The place did not bespeak high rent. He thought back to the war, and the minor deprivations the home folks suffered: rationing of gas and meat, blackouts, curfews. He had been only six or seven when the war started, but his memories of it were sharp. He realized that Kelly had no memory of any real war. Vietnam had ended when she was an infant.

He found her door on the right, and with one more go at his tie knot, pushed the bell that sat in a unit, mid-door.

The door opened so quickly he thought Kelly must have been waiting behind it. Maybe she had even been watching him through the window. The curtains were drawn but she could have peeked.

They stared at each other wordlessly, like shy teenagers.

Kelly spoke first.

"You're early," she exclaimed with nervous excitement, "and I'm ready. I got in the habit of being on time for interviews and shoots. I think it's important, don't you?"

"Oh, yes," Edgar agreed, relieved she had broken the ice.

Kelly was wearing the outfit from the

Playhouse spread—the black velvet skirt that flared around her thin legs and the blue sheer top that fit over some lacy underwear.

"Well, I see you're on time too. I like that. There's nothing worse than sitting around waiting for a date and wondering if he's *ever* going to show up."

"I guess I got in the habit—of being on time, I mean—when I was teaching."

"You were a *teacher*? Wow, I didn't know *that*!"

"Well, I'm not anymore, but I still try to be on time."

"Well, good for you," Kelly said. Then realizing for the first time he was still outside the door and she was still inside, said, "Gosh, where are my manners? Do you want to come in for a minute?"

"It's up to you," he said, looking at his watch. "I guess I have a minute."

"Yes, come meet my roommate, Bambi. She was Treat of the Year for *Playhouse*, you know. I was only Treat of the Month."

Edgar was surprised that when he stepped across the threshold into Kelly's apartment, he could see everything but the bathroom, and

Bambi was standing right there. She must have been waiting there in that spot, listening to their whole conversation. Edgar thought that things that must have sounded okay to the principals on a first date must sound awfully trite to an audience.

"Edgar, this is Bambi."

"Hi, Edgar."

"Hi." Edgar nodded and looked only briefly at the Treat of the Year. She had dressed down for the occasion: jeans and an extra-large sweatshirt. She was definitely not going to be accused of being competitive. Her blonde hair was pulled back. She wore no makeup, and she looked like a show girl on her day off.

Edgar smiled at the booty covering every nook and cranny of the place. "You won a lot of stuff," he said.

"Yeah," Bambi said, "you want to buy a motorcycle, Edgar?"

"Bambi!" Kelly shot at her roommate.

Bambi put her hand to her mouth. "Whoops! Sorry."

"For what?" Edgar asked.

"Oh, nothing," Kelly said.

"How much do you want for it?" Edgar asked.

"Oh, I haven't really checked prices yet," Bambi said. "Do you know what they sell for? It's brand-new."

"No, I'm afraid not."

"Well," Kelly said, glaring at her roommate, "we'd better be on our way—we don't want to lose our table."

"Oh, right," Edgar said.

"Yes," Bambi said simultaneously.

"It was nice to meet you, Bambi," Edgar said.

"Same here."

When Kelly and Edgar got to his car, which was decidedly *not* a sports car, Edgar thought he noticed her disappointment. "Oh, I forgot something—I'll be right back," Kelly said.

As he watched Kelly scamper over the sidewalk and up the steps to her apartment, Edgar got a sudden chill in his chest. Was she deserting him? Had she changed her mind on seeing him? Was he just too old for her? He chided himself for not losing more weight. He was still too fat. Was she let down because he hadn't bought the sports car?

How long should he give her before he went back in to coax her out? He didn't want to seem overly anxious, but fancy places like Pierre Francois have a way of giving your table away if you aren't on time.

He looked at his watch. Fortunately if all went well he had some time to play with. Five minutes, he decided. He would give her five minutes and then he was going after her.

Kelly had stormed back into the apartment.

"Bambi, how *could* you?"

"Sorry, babe, it just slipped out."

"Now there goes our signal."

"You could have said it again. It would be funny."

"So what am I going to say now?"

"Oh, just wink at me, honey. I'll know."

"How about if I say, 'You want a cup of tea, Edgar?'"

"Okay, that's fine."

"Oh, Bambi, isn't he just the sweetest man?"

"Yes, he is, doll," Bambi said. "Now don't keep him waiting, he's liable to drive off."

"Oh, my gosh, you think so?" And Kelly was out the door before Bambi could say, "No."

Kelly came back to the car to see Edgar

checking his watch. "I'm sorry," she said, "did I take too long?"

"No, no, you're fine," he said and started the little car. "I was a little afraid you might not come back," Edgar confessed sheepishly.

"Oh, Edgar, why would I do such a thing?"

"I don't know, changed your mind or something."

"Edgar! I'd do no such thing. I'm really excited about going to Pierre Francois. I've never been, and I hear it's just the *best* place."

"Well, good."

"You wouldn't go pulling a little inferiority complex on me, now would you?"

"No, I..."

"Because I think you are just the *sweetest* man."

"Well, thank you." Edgar blushed. Kelly reached over and patted his arm. It felt good to him.

Through some fairly adroit driving, Edgar was able to pull into the Pierre Francois parking lot in Beverly Hills with minutes to spare. He looked around at the Rolls-Royces parked at the front door, down through the Porsches and Mercedes.

"Look at all these expensive cars," he said. "See how they park them by status? The Rolls next to the door. They'll probably park mine in Arizona."

Kelly let go of her most nervous laugh. "You're funeee," she said.

They were both a little nervous when they presented themselves inside to Jacques, the maître d' in tails. Edgar suspected the kid who parked his car looked condescending, but he wasn't sure. The kid wasn't even Kelly's age—maybe it wasn't his plebeian car but his age advantage over his date's that caused the reaction. And maybe Edgar imagined it.

But, Edgar thought, there is no imagining this maître d'—I can feel the frost right through to my bones.

"Very good, sir," Jacques said, the words seeming to roll off of the end of his razor-sharp nose. "Your table will be ready in a few minutes. If you'd like to wait in the bar, I'll call you."

Edgar got the feeling Jacques was making a visual appraisal of Kelly and found her, as they said in the Bible, wanting.

Edgar didn't want to go to the bar. The dinner, he figured, would probably cost him a

Edgar and Kelly

week's take-home pay and he wasn't keen on paying for a couple ten-dollar drinks—with tax and
tip.

"You want to go to the bar?" he asked
Kelly.

She read his thoughts. "We can wait here.
It's only gonna be a few minutes, he said."

So they hung around the maître d's station and sensed this did not please Jacques.

But there were people all around. It was
Saturday night and the place was jumping.
Jacques would disappear into the main dining
room, then return as Edgar and Kelly expectantly
awaited the nod from this man who held the fate
of their evening in his powerful hands.

It was five minutes after their reservation
time and people were being seated. Edgar was
not at ease in the crowded environment around
the maître d's station, but he still preferred not to
go to the overflowing bar.

The noise bothered Edgar. It wasn't con-
ducive to conversation. Edgar longed to get his
date to the relative privacy of a table. Their dis-
course in this hubbub was limited to smiling at
each other and speculation on when their time
would come to be admitted to the first-class status

of diners at Pierre Francois.

So, instead of making getting-to-know-you talk while they were waiting for their table, Edgar was edgy at the portent of it all. How it must have diminished him in Kelly's eyes. He was obviously being snubbed by the establishment. Did they disapprove of his escort's age? Did they think she came from an escort service?

Kelly was beginning to wonder if she had been recognized and the maître d' was discriminating against her for not being good enough for the place. Something like refusing to seat a woman alone you thought was a hooker. Did he think *she* was a hooker? She had half a mind to go over there and set him straight right now!

Then, about ten minutes later, Edgar saw a couple admitted to the sacred dining room who he thought had come in after he had.

Edgar sauntered over the few steps to the station and looked over Jacques' shoulder at the reservation schedule.

"May I help you, sir?" Jacques asked as a challenge more than a question.

"I was wondering how we were doing," Edgar said, consulting his watch.

"The name, sir."

"Wellington."

"The party at your table has the check. It shouldn't be long."

"I see some party of two below us is crossed out. Are they already seated?"

Edgar pointed. "We are at seven-thirty, here, these people—Barret at seven-forty-five."

"We do only on the half-hour," Jacques said. "They are the same time as you and they were here first."

"You sure?"

Jacques arched an eyebrow. Dare a mortal question him?

Edgar moved back beside Kelly. He smiled at her. She smiled back.

Kelly said, "That maître d' reminds me of so many people who come to this country from other places—and they always give you the feeling their other places where they came from are so superior to this country. I can see it in this guy's face, can't you?"

Edgar nodded.

"You wonder why they stay here."

"Exactly," Edgar said. "Maybe I'm being paranoid, but I don't feel Jacques has our interests at heart, do you?"

"I guess *not!*" she agreed.

Another couple came in from outside and went up to slap Jacques on the back. It was like old-home week. And when they were seated a few minutes later, Edgar began to boil, while Kelly frowned and bit her lower lip. Both felt snubbed. Each felt it was their fault.

When the second couple that came in from the street was ushered to their table by their pal Jacques, Edgar had had enough. He wanted to give the snotty maître d' a piece of his mind.

But Edgar didn't have the talent for it. He was nice as pie on the outside, seething on the inside.

"Look here, sir," Edgar said, "we've been waiting fifty minutes now. We were five minutes early for our reservation and you've seated a lot of people who came after us."

"Yes, I'm sorry, sir, Saturday night is so difficult" — he pronounced it "deefeecoolt." "Your table will not leave."

"Did you ask them to?"

"Oh, no," Jacques said, as though that were unthinkable.

"So seat us at another table."

"Oh, we can't, sir, we are completely booked."

"But tables have come up. We were here first, but you gave them to others."

"They have reserved specific tables, sir."

"Oh, I see—and those specific tables just happened to be empty where my specific table is not."

"I'm afraid so, sir."

Kelly had eased her way up beside Edgar and was raptly following the repartee.

"So, this isn't first come, first served," Kelly chimed in, "you have your special favorites who go ahead of everybody?"

Jacques looked her over as Edgar imagined a slave buyer might have scanned merchandise a hundred and fifty years before—merchandise on which he decided to pass.

"It is the policy of the management, madam. I can do nothing." And he flapped his wings in one of those hopeless gestures.

"So you're telling us you aren't going to seat us, aren't you?"

"No, madam. As soon as the party leaves your table."

"Come on, Edgar—let's get out of here."

Edgar was relieved. "Are you sure?" he asked, hoping she was.

"No, let's go to McDonald's, really. I've had about all the atmosphere I can stand for one night."

They went into the parking lot and gave the ticket to the young attendant. Edgar started fishing in his pocket for a tip.

"Now don't you tip him, Edgar. After the way we've been treated."

"You think if I had slipped old Jacques a twenty we'd be eating now?"

"Oh," Kelly fumed, "I don't doubt that at all. But why should you have to buy your way to a table? You made a reservation. You didn't just drop in on Saturday night. That man was just plain rude. He treated us like dirt."

Edgar had never been able to stiff anyone he thought had the slightest call on a tip. But when the car came and the lad hopped out and held the door open for him, he looked him in the eye and said, "Sorry, no tip, we waited almost an hour and never got our table."

The attendant looked stunned. When Edgar and Kelly were in the car, he slapped the back fender and said, "Thanks, sporty!"

It would take Edgar approximately three weeks to get over that insult.

"Phew!" Kelly said as they drove off. "I won't miss *that* place."

"Where to?" Edgar asked her.

"Why not McDonald's? Let's just go to the opposite end of the ladder and let our hair down and have a good time. What do you say? Game?"

"Game," he said. "Now you gotta show me where the closest one is."

"Okay." She was happy. She clapped her hands to prove it. "Take a left at the next light."

KELLY AND EDGAR

While the doors were open, you could always find people at McDonald's. A little before nine on a Saturday night there was still plenty of activity, but a table was available in the back.

"Whoeee!" Kelly said, "we got a table without a maître d'."

Edgar smiled. He found her simple, down-to-earth personality so engaging.

Being gun shy, table-wise, they took the

Kelly and Edgar

woodgrain Formica table, sans tablecloth, with the oxford-brown plastic swing-out seats even before they ordered. Both having the same idea, they pounced on the table, sat facing each other, then when it sunk in they both burst out laughing.

"Imagine being stoked about getting a table at McDonald's," Kelly said, laughing her energetic laugh.

"I guess we shouldn't wait for a waiter," Edgar said, turning around to make sure there wasn't one headed their way.

They were at a window which looked out on the busy parking lot.

"Do you come here often?" Edgar asked.

"Pretty often."

"What do you recommend?"

"Oh, I just adore their Big Mac...and fries. Cokes are pretty good too."

"Sounds good," Edgar said, rising from the plastic seat. He looked at Kelly and thought how lovely she looked here. So much more at ease than in the artificial environment of Pierre Francois.

"You'll be here when I get back?" he said, and felt foolish for it.

She was startled at first, then said, "You *are* coming back?"

He smiled and winked at her. She winked back.

While he was standing in line, Edgar thought he should perhaps have the fish or the Chicken McNuggets—and maybe a Diet Coke, but by the time he got to the perky uniformed girl at the computer-driven order station, he decided that would be antisocial, and might even make Kelly self-conscious.

When Edgar arrived back with his bounty overflowing the tray, Kelly was nowhere in sight. His heart sank and he slid the tray on the table and looked the three hundred and sixty degrees. Then he realized he was being silly. How would she get home, hitchhike? Taxi? She didn't blame him for the Pierre Francois fiasco. She couldn't have been a better sport about it.

Just as he was struggling to reassure himself, Kelly came bounding around the corner and flounced herself with an engaging abandon onto the plastic.

She looked at Edgar and giggled. "Just made some room for getting down to some serious eating. Mmm," she said, eying the goodies, "looks yummy." With her fingers she stuck a couple of French fries in her mouth and, with exaggerated gestures, licked her fingers, one at a time.

"Take *that*, Pierre Francois," she said, with a flourish of her licked-clean hand.

Edgar took a bite of his Mac. "Hmm," he said. "Now this is eating."

"Right on," she said, taking a bite of hers. "None of that sissy French food."

"And the whole thing cost less than one dessert at that stuffed-shirt place," Edgar said. "I saved so much money I want to buy you something," he said. "You pick."

"Oh, Edgar, you don't have to do any such thing."

"Well, I want to—so you be thinking."

Kelly looked at Edgar with a liquid admiration in her eyes. "I swear, Edgar, you are just the nicest man."

"And when I entertain a date," he said, waving his Big Mac in the air, "I pull out all the stops."

"I'm so glad we're here, Edgar," she said. "It's so nice of you to take me out."

"Oh, no, it's nice of you to *go* out with me. I'll bet you have lots of dates." He wanted to add "with people your own age," but he checked himself.

"No, I don't have a lot of dates, not at all."

"Why not?"

She wrinkled her cute nose. "I don't know. Sometimes I think maybe I showed too much. You know, in *Playhouse*. So it's hard to find serious men, you know?"

"That's too bad," Edgar said, but he thought it was good. "You didn't show too much for me."

"Oh, Eddie!" She touched his arm with the lightest push.

"Really. Maybe the world would be in less of a fix if everybody were photographed like that—from leaders on down."

"Really? You mean that? Like the President and all?"

"Well—" he hesitated—"maybe not."

"Oh, Eddie," she giggled, "you're funeee, I swear! Is it all right if I call you Eddie?"

"Sure. I like it," he said. "Nobody ever called me that before."

"Really? Not even your mother?"

He shook his head.

"Well, I think it fits you."

"How so?"

"You're all cuddly like. Oh, dear—I'm sorry, does that embarrass you?"

"Not at all," Edgar said. "I like it." He paused to visualize what "cuddly" looked like.

"A penny for your thoughts," she said.

Edgar grinned. "I was just wondering if cuddly wasn't synonymous with fat?"

"Well, it is *not*!" she said. "I don't think you're fat. I mean, I've seen a lot fatter."

"Thanks," he said, "I think. I've been trying to work it off—so you wouldn't have to be seen in a fancy French restaurant with an overweight baboon. I took off thirty-five pounds since we met."

"Really, Eddie, that's great!"

"Didn't get us a table though," he laughed.

"I'm glad," Kelly said. "I really do like this much better." She threw in another fry. "I'm impressed you lost all that weight."

"Yeah, you get the credit."

"Oh, Eddie, you're *so* nice."

"No, really. Tonight I almost bought the chicken and Diet Coke, but I thought, what the heck, this is a celebration."

"Yeah!" Kelly exclaimed. "Hey, you know what I heard on the television?"

"What?"

"That an order of fettucini Alfredo had more fat in it than three Big Macs."

"Hm," Edgar said. "All that cream, I guess."

"And that's what I'da had at Pierre Francois, so I think I'll just have two more Big Macs and I'll still be ahead of the game."

"I'll be happy to get them for you—but I hope you won't mind if I don't join you." Edgar passed his hands over his midsection. "I still have this tire..."

"Love handles we call it." Kelly smiled in that down-home, wouldn't-hurt-a-fly smile.

Edgar was enchanted—and surprised. It was an expression he had not heard before.

"Tell me about your work," he said. "Do you enjoy it?"

"Well, yes, I do. I could not work inside at a desk all day long. I just could *not*."

"Is that true what I read in the magazine? Did you say those things?"

"*Playhouse* is pretty good about printing what you say," she said. "They aren't all."

"So you really said you liked people to admire your body?"

"Sure I do. We all like to be admired, well, don't we?"

"I guess."

"And you've got to be admired for what you *can* be admired for. I like people to admire my body," Kelly said, getting one of those sheepish grins on her face, "not much chance I'd be admired for my mind."

Edgar wanted to argue but it took him too long. "You can be admired for your person," he said at last, "your delightful nature, your generous friendship."

"Oh, wow," she said, "I put out a long pole *that* time."

"Pole?"

"Yeah, to fish for your compliments," Kelly said.

"Oh, no—I meant it."

"Well, thank you."

Edgar noted she didn't drop her eyelashes. There was no *faux* demure about Kelly. She was of this earth. A trooper—a young girl on her own. There wasn't time for the luxuries of playing games.

"So what kinds of jobs have you gotten lately?" Edgar asked.

"I just did a calendar for a tool company. I modeled in a trade show for a motorcycle manufacturer. I get lots of nude offers, but I only do the art nudes. I did a shower scene for a shower-head company."

"What is an art nude—as opposed to a non-art nude?" Edgar asked.

"Oh, you can tell that easy. When they want you to do porn poses—like *Hustler* magazine, where it's just *raw*, you know—that's where I draw the line."

"So you think *Playhouse* is art stuff?"

"Well, I do. I'm alone in those—showing my body—all of it, I admit, but I don't have any dogs or horses licking me, you know—I'm not doin' it."

"Looked like your hand was doing something."

"Oh, that. Well, I wasn't. My hand was just there. You know, there are subtle differences. You like to look at them, don't you?"

"Oh, yes."

"Do you look at *Hustler*?"

"Well, I wouldn't not look at it—but I

don't much, no," Edgar said.

"Why not?"

Edgar frowned. "I see what you mean. *Playhouse* is a little more artistic. But come on," he said playfully, "tell the truth, were you posing there because you thought it was artistic? I mean, do you take off your clothes for art—or for the money?"

Kelly's smile was that of the guilty child, fessing up; charming in its guileless candor. "I expect it was for the money."

"Have you turned down other jobs because you thought they weren't art?"

"Well, yes I have."

"Will you always be able to?"

Kelly didn't answer right away. Her brow creased. "I've thought about that. I'm twenty-three and things are going okay. I mean, I haven't been on the cover of *Sports Illustrated* or anything, but I'm getting by. I haven't had to make too many compromises, and knock wood," she tapped her head, "I won't have to. I've made up my mind I'll be an Avon lady before I do porn or hook."

"Hook?"

"You know, be a hooker. Now, Edgar," she

cocked an eye sternly at him, "surely you know what a hooker is?"

"Yes." He dropped his eyelids.

"I'm so relieved. At least you aren't *that* innocent."

"No," Edgar said. "Tell me, what's it like being in *Playhouse?* I don't mean the shoot—I guess that's much like the one I was at..."

"Pretty much."

"I mean the aftereffects. People's reactions."

"You get all kinds, really. Some people, you know, never mention it. Then you get the kooks. I'm scared to death of the kooks—the guys who fall in love with your picture and decide to express that love by shooting you."

"So how do you protect yourself against that?"

"First of all they used another name for me. The magazine will not give out any information except through my agent. I mean, I don't want to turn away any legitimate offers."

"Do guys try to date you through your agent?"

"Oh, yeah. And they have all kinds of creative approaches—like they are old friends or classmates of mine. I wonder what they think if I don't recognize their name I'm going to be so embarrassed I'll say, 'Oh, sure,' and go out with them. Or they'll say I just called them but they lost my phone number."

"I guess agents earn their money."

"You bet they do!" Kelly agreed.

Edgar was contorting his brain to make himself come off better than the regular Joe who fell in love with her picture. He decided he had not been smitten until he had seen her in person. He tried to explain it just that way to Kelly, but she waved him off.

"Oh, you don't have to tell me that, Eddie. You're a dear, sweet man and I'm just so lucky to know you. Face it," she said, "I'm just not used to gentlemen like you, Eddie, unless they are queers or something."

Edgar blushed. He began to wonder if she wasn't patronizing his age. He hadn't set out to be a surrogate grandfather to the girl, and now he was beginning to wonder if that were how she pictured him.

"Have you ever gone out with one of these guys who saw you somewhere and calls your agent?" Edgar asked.

The Real Sleeper

"No way! It's *way* too scary, the things that are happening nowadays to girls—and even little boys. I mean, do you see all that stuff on television about all the molesting and even the churches and all? Isn't that depressing? Celibacy just isn't normal, no way. I think they should let those priests marry, then they wouldn't have to go after kids. What do you think, Eddie?"

"I think you're right."

"I mean, I'm no prude," she explained, "I *love* sex and all, but I do think it's wrong to do it with these young, innocent kids—it's really disgusting. I mean, I wouldn't mind if these perverts went after each other—but little kids!" She shuddered. "No wonder this country is all hung up about sex."

"Just this country?"

"I don't know, the whole world maybe. The Muslim countries, I guess, and the Catholics—but I don't know, it seems some of these other countries like France and Sweden are not so weird, don't you think?"

Edgar thought. Then he thought some more. From repression, he thought, who should know better?

"You don't want to answer?" Kelly asked.

"Or are you thinking?"

"I'm thinking. I know someone who is....very repressed. I just wonder what percentage. Has it improved? Have things loosened up in..."—he was about to say "*your* generation"— "the modern generation?"

"Well, I guess they *have*," Kelly said with bulging eyes. "Of course, then we got AIDS to scare the shit out of everyone."

"Does it scare you?"

"Well, sure—yes and no. I wouldn't be afraid of you, for instance, but you never know who you're with."

Edgar was touched by her confidence. Then he wondered if it were a compliment or a sad commentary on his innocence.

"So I try to stay away from the druggies and homos. I mean, when you think about it there just aren't many straights dropping over from it, you know. I think the guy who says it's that drugs causes AIDS might be right—what do you think?"

"I don't know. Plausible as the other, I guess. We admit smoking kills, and alcohol kills, but we seem reluctant to say drugs could cause AIDS."

"That's because sex diseases are more dramatic. Bigger headlines. Sell more papers. 'Cause *everyone* does sex, but only the dorks do drugs."

"You ever?" he asked.

"Never," she said. "Oh! Smoked a joint once at a party—trying to be cool, I guess...but I didn't inhale." They both got a good hoot about that.

There was nothing left on the table but McDonald's copious product wrappings: a sea of cardboard, waxed paper, cups and bags, most of it imprinted with the scintillating symbol of the golden arches. But, there was no pause in their seamless conversation. Time was ticking by as it inexorably does, but you would never know it to watch this pair at the back table.

The flow of words was not staunched; their interest never flagged.

"What about *your* job?" Kelly said a little while later.

"Not very exciting," he said, "pleasant enough, I guess." Then he gave her his history from Rutgers on, soft-pedaling his wife's involvement.

Kelly stared into his eyes as she listened.

Kelly and Edgar

Edgar was not used to so much attention from anyone when he spoke. It was giving him a heady feeling.

"But do you like what you do?" she asked at last. "With the books and all?"

"Well, I suppose. Could be doing a lot worse things," Edgar said.

"Now, Eddie, is that an answer?"

"I guess I don't think about liking it much. I just do it. You know, I'm a pretty old guy and things take on a different perspective with age."

"Well, you don't *look* old, Eddie. If I thought you were an old man, I wouldn't call you Eddie—'Mr. Wellington,' I'd say, or *maybe* if I felt real comfortable with you—as I *do*—I might call you Edgar."

Edgar smiled; he couldn't remember when he had smiled so much. Probably never. Then he realized the last time he smiled like this. It was when he met Kelly. Was it remotely possible that what was happening to him was what they wrote all those sonnets about, all those soupy songs and silly woman's magazine stories? And the lion's share of what he taught in Am Lit in the old days and the vast majority of what the

Oak Tree Press published. Who was he kidding? This was not what he set out to do, surely. He had set out to prove his manhood, to demonstrate conclusively that though he was irrefutably entering old age, he could still be young.

No, that's not it, he thought. That's textbook psychiatry. That's not me. I can't believe that I'm really getting a soft spot for this dear, dear, uneducated girl. It's a cinch I could never talk Melville with her unless she saw the movie. I've got to be crazy. Three times her age — and look at her. She actually seems to *like* me. How could I take advantage of her — get her hopes up?

The faithful and steady clientele was filtering out of McDonald's, but the odd couple at the back table was not aware of it.

Edgar was touched by Kelly's saying he didn't look old — as if she meant it.

"You're some girl," he said, and she lit up and reached her hands across the table to touch his.

"What a nice thing to say," she said.

"You don't mind me saying 'girl'? I guess I should say 'woman' if I wanted to keep up with the times."

"Say anything you want," Kelly said, "I

Kelly and Edgar

love anything you say about me."

"Really?"

"Sure. It's like admiration—my body, you know. But you're different."

"How so?"

"Oh, I get the feeling you are a real good person. I just feel so comfortable with you."

"Like an old shoe," he laughed.

"Now, Eddie," she remonstrated, "if you keep talking about being old, soon you will be. You are what you think you are."

Her pop psychology, which Edgar realized would have been so annoying coming from someone else, warmed him and stimulated him like he was being exposed to a fresh, revolutionary idea.

How easy it is, he thought, to take a fancy to someone for sometimes the narrowest reason, then to quickly, groundlessly, ascribe to them all sorts of sterling and endearing qualities. Which qualities, of course, rapidly vanish, leaving you to wonder what made you think they existed in the first place.

Kelly hugged herself. "I just feel so good," she said. "I feel like that bird," she said, transported back in time.

The Real Sleeper

"What bird?" Edgar asked, looking out on the parking lot as though there might be a bird out there in the middle of the night.

Kelly spoke, becalmed at the memory.

"I was out at the beach doing a shoot for this swimsuit company and all of a sudden the wind came up something fierce. It was so windy we had to shut down and sit in our cars until it let up.

"There was a bird over the water who just hung on the wind out there—he just had his wings out and he was just hanging in the same exact place. Every once in a while he'd flap those big wings of his to stay up, I guess, but he wasn't going anywhere, you know what I mean?"

Edgar said he did. Oh, boy, he thought, do I? I've had my wings out with the wind in my face like that for more than thirty years. Is she telling me she feels that way too?

Kelly went on. "I guess if I were more long-term-goal oriented I would think that bird was about not ever getting anywhere—you know, the forces of the wind and nature and society and all, just keeping you from getting ahead. But I don't. I am so content that time itself just stands still and I just hang in the air and let the wind do the work."

"Is that what you feel like now?"

"Yeah."

"I guess I do too," Edgar said.

Kelly broke into a broad smile. "I feel almost giddy," she said. "Like I'm high on Coke—and not the powder."

"Not even the diet," he said.

"Yeah."

Neither Kelly nor Edgar realized it, but a McDonald's night manager was standing over them. He cleared his throat and Kelly looked up, then Edgar. They were confused at first. Why was this guy standing there? Then, on looking around, they saw, while they had been wrapped up in each other, the place had cleared out.

"It's closing time," the manager said. "Have to lock up. Hope you'll come again."

"Gee—closing? Really?" They stood up, dazed, as though someone had awakened them from a sound sleep.

They drove back to Kelly's place in relative silence. Finally Kelly broke it. "I had a really good time," she said. "You are such good company, Eddie."

"So are you. It was a lot of fun. Gee, it

sure got late without me realizing it."

"Me neither. See, time really does fly when you're having fun," Kelly said.

"Like sex," Edgar said.

"Yeah."

"That's what you said at the photo session for the book cover, remember?"

"I did? No!" Kelly said. "Well, I guess I could've," she laughed, and he joined her.

"You did," he said.

There was another moment of silence.

"Gee, it's awful late for you to drive all the way home, Eddie," Kelly said. "Would you like to stay over?"

"Would I?" he said, thinking how that had been his goal all along. But now that the offer was there, out in the open—on the table—he didn't know what to say.

When he pulled in front of her house, he had to park in a red zone, so he left the motor running.

"Oh, it was *real* fun," she said. "Will you come in for a minute? Or more?"

Conflicting emotions and errant thoughts were swirling in Edgar's head. Here it was, the offer he had dreamed of, the opportunity he had worked toward with single-minded resolve, and yet he was sitting here as though he had been bronzed like a baby shoe.

"I..." Edgar began, but stopped. "You..." He couldn't get his thoughts into words because he didn't have much idea what his thoughts were. "Kelly," he said, "I...I really like you a lot."

"That's so nice, Eddie."

"No, it's nothing special—why wouldn't anybody like you? You're just a great person." Edgar was having trouble. Kelly sensed it, but didn't know how to help him. "The thing is, see, I wanted...I mean, what I originally had in mind was...with you, I mean...was, well, you know, maybe going to bed. In the beginning. You were just such a free spirit, like I never met, and here I was, getting pretty old—so old, I was beginning to think my loving days were about gone."

"Now, Eddie, no more old talk."

"Yes, I forgot. But, Kelly, you know I am way too old for you—I'm—"

She put her fingers on his lips. "You aren't old to me. I don't care if you're a hundred. It wouldn't make any difference."

"You're too good to be true."

"Oh, B.S."

"You're really sweet," he said. "The thing is, I didn't expect to fall for you like this, and I literally don't know what's happening to me. One part of me wants to come in with you right now and just do whatever happens—but the other part—the repressed part that's been with me all my life—is holding me back. Not because I don't want to, but because it just isn't my nature to do anything so fast. See, I think good things take time. When I see something in a store I want to buy, I never buy it while I'm there. I go home and think about it—usually I go back and get it."

"You don't have to buy me, Eddie."

"No, no, I didn't mean that. Oh, I guess I'm not too articulate about this—it was better when we were talking about birds staying still in the wind."

Now, Kelly O'Leary, Kelly said to herself, you don't be too anxious about this, you hear? This is a nice man who doesn't have a lot of experience, and I do not want you scaring him half to death. Just go slow!

"You're doing fine," Kelly said. "I understand completely. It's too soon for you. You need to think, and I *do* understand."

"You're very kind."

Kelly and Edgar

"No, I'm not. Me, I thought already. But I don't want to push you. I certainly do *not*," Kelly said. "And I can take it if you aren't sure you like me enough."

"Oh, no, hey, no! That's not it. The problem is I think I like you too much."

Kelly was thoroughly confused and her pretty face showed it.

"How about if we both sleep on it?" he asked.

"Great!" She smiled. "Here?"

Edgar smiled back. "No, not here. If I were in there with you, I don't think there would be much thinking going on."

"I see what you mean—more *feeling* than thinking..."

"Yeah." Edgar was in a daze. Kelly was afraid he'd fall asleep at the wheel.

"Well, if you're sure, Eddie. But it's so late. You could have my bed and I could sleep on the floor till you've had time to think."

"I'd better go."

"Don't you need coffee first?"

"No, I'm okay."

"You sure you won't fall asleep at the wheel or anything?"

"Yeah, sure," Edgar said. "I'll call you tomorrow. Will it be okay if I come again tomorrow?"

"You bet it will! I'll be waiting." She looked at her apartment window. "Gee, I guess we're a little late for Bambi. I hope she's not still up."

"You think she would be?"

"She was going to go to Sheri's—but it's so late, she probably just fell asleep."

"That's another reason I should go home."

"Well, I do have some privacy in the loft—but she'll go if I ask her, I know she will. I've done it for her," she said, then decided that sounded like they were running a business. "Not often," she added.

Edgar smiled. "I'll call," he said.

"Promise?"

"Promise."

She leaned over and kissed him softly on the lips. And before he opened his eyes, she was out of the car.

Edgar thought he should have taken her to the door, but decided he wouldn't have been able to resist going in. Instead he watched until she opened the door, turned and blew him a kiss, then closed the door behind her.

He drove off very slowly.

Inside, Kelly found a note on the motorcycle seat from Bambi:

> *Kel: Went to Sheri's. Thought it*
> *was a sure thing. Oh, by the way, ask*
> *Edgar if he wants to buy a motorcycle.*
> *Good luck,*
> *Bam*

EDGAR

Driving home, listlessly preoccupied, I had the sense I was driving in the wrong direction. I never had developed a competent sense of direction, but now, though I had traveled this freeway from L.A. to Thousand Oaks countless times, I had the strongest urge to turn around.

I was a fool for leaving Kelly. With every mile I put between us, I felt the bigger fool. By the time I turned off the 101 at my exit, I was convinced I was an utter moron.

I had begun this relationship thinking Kelly was not terribly bright. Now I thought *I* was the dummy. Why in the world did I drive away? Was it a lifelong pattern I just couldn't break? Was there something defective in me? Was I the victim of an outmoded sense of chivalry?

I approached the house I had driven home to for almost twenty years. For all that time it had been a familiar landmark, an anchor to me. Now it seemed strange and unfamiliar, as though I had turned into the wrong driveway. The house did not send out a welcoming beacon but seemed a fortress against me.

Come on, I chided myself, you're delirious from lack of sleep. It's almost three in the morning.

But inside the house, I felt more an alien in unfriendly territory. I often felt alone in the house, even when Penelope was in residence, but now it was as though all the spirits that once made it a home had deserted it and I felt I was in the center of a barren warehouse in a land where no one spoke my language.

In spite of the punishingly late hour, I was angry, but not sleepy. Angry with myself for walking away from another opportunity—and those opportunities would get fewer and fewer as I slipped into my dotage.

No more, I thought, no more. *Carpe diem.*

As I was dialing the phone, I realized how stupidly thoughtless it was for me to call a girl I just left an hour before—in the middle of the night.

Well, if she doesn't pick it up on the first ring, I vowed, I'm hanging up.

"Hello!" she said before the first ring completed.

"Were you asleep?"

"No, I was laying here thinking about you," she said. "I was looking at the clock and trying to figure out how far you had driven. I just couldn't sleep for thinking about you."

"I didn't want to wake you."

"You didn't. I was hoping you'd call."

"But, I thought you were the great sleeper."

She laughed. "Yes, but not so much when I'm excited."

"Me neither," I said. "I may never go to sleep."

Edgar

"Edgar?"

"Hm?"

"Do you feel like I do?"

"Hm?"

"Like we should be together?"

"Sleeping, you mean?"

"Well, yeah, eventually, I guess, we'd go to sleep."

"Yeah."

"Well, would you, I mean, if you want, you could come back."

Oh, my God, I thought. Oh, yes. Yes, yes, yes. But I said, "What about your roommate?"

"She's not here."

"Oh."

"Want to?"

Now all of my ordinary thought mechanisms ground to a dead stop. My heart was still pumping, but my mind was a blank. My staid, inhibited rationale, usually so close at hand, had deserted me.

"It's three in the morning," I heard myself say—that old, unwanted reason pushing to the fore.

"And you could be here by four—maybe earlier, this time of night."

"Yeah."

There was a silence while my heart battled my mind.

Kelly said, "We could just cuddle, if that's all you wanted."

It sounded good to me. She was so considerate. She wanted someone to hold her, I realized. And I did too.

"I'll be there," I said.

"Good!"

I was backing the car out of the driveway and nosing it down the hill before I realized what I was doing.

Then my motions seemed effortless. Driving the car was automatic and unconscious. My thoughts were fifty miles ahead of me.

A touch of the old caution returned as I saw my speedometer nosing up to ninety miles per hour. It was impossible to tell if those cars behind you were cops, and I didn't relish getting a ticket at three-thirty a.m. and trying to explain it to Penelope.

Then I thought, how foolish. Here I am, still worrying about Penelope on my way to a woman who has made me feel better in one platonic evening than Penelope has in our whole marriage.

Did Penelope ever do anything on all these trips she went on? Maybe other men appealed to her more than I did.

I stepped on the gas and the needle went over ninety. Suddenly, I took my foot from the gas pedal when I thought how much it would slow me down to get a ticket.

The old doubts exploded to the surface like a volcano on a sunny afternoon. What am I doing? I'm almost sixty years old! What if I *can't* do anything? What about the girl? Normally they want a commitment. What can I give? Didn't I make a pledge—a marriage vow to Penelope to forsake all others? Sure, it's more honored in the breach, but not by me.

So, maybe it's time.

And maybe you are kidding yourself—a realist giving himself over to a fantasy.

Should I turn back? I wondered. But that would be cruel to Kelly. I was beyond the point of no return. I could always just go and explain my doubts to Kelly. She would understand. Perhaps that is what I should do.

But then the picture of Kelly sitting across

from me at the plastic table at McDonald's burst into my head. She looked so strong yet so vulnerable, so sophisticated yet so innocent that I couldn't wait to take her in my arms, and when I left the freeway at Santa Monica my heart was pumping wildly. The sound of my blood banging through that indispensable organ scared me. What if it burst right here? What if it burst while I was in Kelly's arms? Fantasies were popping off in my head like firecrackers. My doubts slowly disappeared, my mind eased into a comfortable focus on Kelly.

KELLY AND EDGAR

The lights were low when Kelly opened the door. Edgar could see the central red, white and blue motorcycle all right, but the premium prizes against the wall were shadowy creatures laying in wait for some enlivening excitement.

Kelly had on a silky maroon robe. It was one of Bambi's prizes and she had borrowed it. She liked the feel of it on her skin and wished she could afford something like it sometime.

"Oh, Eddie," she said when she opened the door, "thanks so much for coming."

"Thanks for having me."

She stretched her hands out to him. With a tentative motion, he put his arm around her and kissed her on the cheek, as he had done at the photography studio. Then he slid his other arm around her and they stood motionless, locked in that embrace as though they were dancing without moving. Like that bird on the wind.

"You feel so nice."

"You too," Edgar said. "You are so good to me."

"No, no," she purred, "don't say that. I am not good to you. You are good to me."

"Can't we be good to each other?"

"Okay."

She was so warm against him. Her skin was so smooth, smoother than he ever thought skin could be. "It's uncanny," he muttered.

"What is?"

"Your skin—how can it be so smooth? You are so perfect."

"Nah," she cooed, but she was pleased, he could feel that.

Kelly and Edgar

His hand found her hair and it was silk. He thought all hair was straw—it had taken him sixty years to find silk. He couldn't remove his hand from her silk.

"Shall we lie down?" she asked.

"Hmm?" Edgar's receptors were off duty. "Oh," he said. "On the motorcycle?"

She giggled.

"What's so funny?"

"That was my signal."

"What?"

"My signal to Bambi that you would stay with me." She was speaking over his shoulder—in a dreamy voice. "I'd say, 'Edgar, do you want to buy a motorcycle?' but she said it first—before we went out."

"Was she here when you came in?"

"No," she said. "She decided you were a sure thing—all *she* knew."

"Yeah."

"I'm so glad you came back."

"Me too."

"We could go to my loft."

"Okay."

Edgar followed her up the ladder and saw that underneath that maroon silk robe, Kelly was just as she was for the book cover.

In the loft they hugged again in virtually the only space left to them after the bed and prizes were in place. It was not a sudden action, but rather a dissolving that eased them onto the bed, sitting at first then reclining, then happily horizontal.

The silky feel of the sheets startled Edgar.

"What are these sheets?" he asked.

"Satin," she said. "Bambi won them..."

"Lot of great prizes," Edgar said.

"Yeah," she said as they slid down together, holding each other as though time had stopped the universe. Their universe was two. Two out of five billion lonely souls. Two who felt they found the answer.

There was no rush to the ultimate intimacy. The gentle stroking was more learning and exploring than it was explosive at first. To Kelly it seemed so luxuriously long until she felt his hand inside her robe.

She stifled a giggle. "Why, Eddie, you're still all dressed. Do you go to bed with all your clothes on?"

"No."

"Shall I help you?"

"That would be so nice."

She unbuttoned and pulled and slid and lifted until he pressed against her unencumbered.

He kissed the side of her neck. She kissed his ear.

Then somehow, very slowly, their lips found each other and met without pressure and they lay there touching lips and stroking bodies as though their passion was the suspension of that bird and some unseen and gentle force of nature would move them in the right direction at the right time.

Without pressure, the tongues began exploring the lips and mouths, until finally, eons later, their movements quickened, their explorations heated until there was no rationale left in either mind—the souls were moving, the spirits in charge.

"Are you...birth controlled?" he asked.

"Mmm—pill."

"There *is* someone?"

"No. You just never know...when you'll get lucky...like now...Mmm."

"Mmmm."

"Be part of me," she said.

"Oh....." And by mutual balletic and gentle slow-motion moves of a pair of dancers, he was.

"Oooo—you're a *big* part," she cooed.

His fears of dilapidating manhood vanished. His heart exploded with a passionate sense of paradise. At last, he thought. At last.

"Oh, that feels so good," Kelly said.

"Oh, yes," he said.

"Oh, nice—"

"Nice."

She moved, she purred, she cooed. She kissed him, she stroked him, she did all the things he'd dreamed about all his life. Simple things so foreign to Penelope as to be finally unimaginable to Edgar. But the best thing was she actually seemed to enjoy it. She was as transported as he was.

Oh, he thought, if I have a heart attack right here I will have finally achieved true happiness.

They had together muscular rhythms so neither was aware who was doing and who was done to. It was like a symphony of fluid movements, a concerto where the artist was accompanying the orchestra and Kelly and Edgar took

Kelly and Edgar

turns being the artist.

They murmured to each other profound truths that they knew would be terribly trite in the light of day. Superlatives abounded.

Kelly could do things with hidden muscles Edgar had never even imagined. She made him feel like a god who could command supernatural sensuality with the mere passing of a hand through her hair. For the first time in his life he felt complete: completely satisfied and completely content. And they lay together with nothing between them: no false inhibitions, no debilitating defenses. Two creatures as uncomplicated by worldly sophistication as is the most basic force in nature. They were lovers pure, and lovers simple, completely satisfying and completely compensating.

"Eddie," the soft voice of Kelly floated into his reverie.

"Hm?"

"Can you stay here forever?"

"Ah. Mm. I was afraid you wouldn't ask."

Then at the peak of their unguarded passion, thunder and lightning struck them simultaneously, like the apocalypse, bursting the tender bubble of shared tension, fulfilling the luscious promise of their strained, glistening bodies.

It was as if the god of Eros was saying, "Ecstasy is temporal. Slow your breathing, calm your hearts, be content in sublime repose. Enough." And enough it was. More than enough, and they lay glued together now by the fluids created by their own special bodies, not caring if they ever moved again.

All sense of time had escaped them both. Neither felt like breaking the spell with words.

But someone had to speak first unless they mutually agreed to a life of silence, and the way they felt holding each other, that didn't seem like such a bad idea.

It was Kelly who put the merest crimp in their idyllic silence.

"Oh, Eddie, you are so great. I've never been loved like this in my life."

"Oh, Kelly," he said, his tone skeptical in spite of wanting to believe her.

"No, it's true," she said. "I have absolutely never felt like this before in my life. Men just aren't so considerate of a woman's feelings as you, Eddie. It's just the most wonderful feeling in the world." And she snuggled to get in the small space under his arm.

"I've never felt this way either," Edgar admitted.

"Really?"

The sun had come up in the sky and the light was peeking in on the naked, entwined couple in the loft of the simple apartment Kelly, the Treat of the Month, shared with Bambi, the Treat of the Year.

"You know what I'm thinking?" Edgar said.

"Hmm?"

"I'm thinking if I don't live another day, you will have given me something that was worth waiting sixty years for."

"Sixty years?" she said. "What do you mean? You aren't sixty years old. No way."

"Why, what did you think I was?"

"Maybe forty-five. I'm not good with ages."

He indulged in a light chuckle. "I guess not." Then he was suddenly taken back. "Will you still like me now that you know how really old I am?"

"Why, Edgar Wellington," she said, propping herself up on an elbow, "how in the world could you ask that after the nicest love we have either ever had? Do you think I'd care if you were a hundred and sixty? Does that mean that you couldn't love someone who was only a child of twenty-three?"

"I just did," he said, and drew her close.

"Anyway," she said, "don't let's hear any more of that dying talk, it's such a downer."

"Sorry."

In time, Edgar wondered, would that turn into an argument? How long would paradise stick around?

Kelly stroked his chest. "Eddie," she said, "you look like you are deep in thought. Are they happy thoughts?"

"Oh—"

"Because happy thoughts are all you are allowed to have now, okay?"

"Okay," he said. "I just feel like sharing every thought I've ever had with you. But, I have to do some editing if you want to hear only the happy thoughts. 'Cause before I met you, I didn't have that many happy thoughts."

"Happy thoughts," she reiterated, and put her lips to his—for about twenty minutes, until the phone rang.

Edgar had the annoying sensation that

Kelly and Edgar

the telephone would be Penelope.

"Let's not answer it," he said, still blissful in the arms of his angel.

"It's probably just Bambi. Good Lord, what time is it getting to be anyway?"

The phone kept ringing by Kelly's bed.

"It's probably tomorrow," Edgar said. "Maybe next week for all I know." But how would Penelope know the phone number? he wondered.

With a minimum of disengagement, Kelly reached for the phone on the floor beside her bed.

"Hello," she answered with a low, throaty sound distinguishable only because it was the expected salutation. "Oh, hi, Bambi...real fine...wonderful, thanks...Yes, he is...Could you?...just a couple more eons...no, I'm joking, but I'd be grateful for anything...Knock first, please. Okay, thanks so much, Bam, you're a dear."

When she hung up, she moved back to her lover. "Umm — Bambi's gonna call again in four hours."

"Not enough," Edgar said.

"Not nearly," she said.

"Kelly?"

"Hm?"

"Did I hear you say 'Good Lord' when the phone rang?"

"I don't know, why?"

"Oh, it just hit me that your language is, well, a lot tamer than it was when I met you..."

She wrinkled her nose. "Well, naturally..."

"Naturally? Why?"

"Because I could sense your refinement. I didn't think you cared for that gutter talk."

"You mean you changed for me? Just like that?"

"Well, yes, I did too!"

Edgar drew Kelly closer in the silence of their pounding hearts. Another eternity passed before Edgar muttered something about an obligation to fuel their bodies.

"Breakfast?" Kelly asked. "Maybe tomorrow—or the next day."

"Okay," he said.

"Where shall we go?" Kelly said, then changed her mind. "No, I don't want to go."

"I don't either, but I think we'll faint."

"*I* know," she said, "let's go back to McDonald's."

Kelly and Edgar

They dressed each other, very slowly. Edgar tried to replicate the motions he remembered from the book-cover shoot, but he slowed his movements considerably.

In the car she snuggled up to him in the way he had wondered if anyone ever would.

"Let's get the same table," she said.

"Great idea."

The table was taken.

"Let's wait," she said. "They move fast here."

"Okay."

They tried to be unobtrusive, standing by the wall and keeping their eye on the table. The two teenage girls were uncomfortably aware they were being watched. Edgar noted they were pretty girls after whom he might have lusted B.K.— before Kelly. But now his interest was solely in possessing the inanimate table.

A young family, father, mother and two-year-old child, vacated the table next to the girls, so Kelly and Edgar sat, without taking their eye from the prize. The girls at the back table were becoming noticeably uneasy at the attention and finally stood in a huff and glared as Edgar and Kelly dashed for their table.

The Real Sleeper

"Weirdos," one of the girls said, looking over her shoulder at Edgar and Kelly.

"Totally," her companion agreed.

But Edgar and Kelly were staring deep into each other's bleary eyes and holding hands across the table.

Edgar broke the silence. He seemed to be the hungriest. "What'll you have?"

"Oh, gosh, I don't know," she said, "I've never been here for breakfast. What do they have?"

"Egg McMuffin," he said, "and stuff like that. I don't eat breakfast out much. Usually just coffee and toast at home."

"I know what," Kelly said, "I'm going to have just what I had last night. It was so perfect I want to do it again."

"A Big Mac? For breakfast?"

"Why not? I still have two to go to do the damage of one fettucini Alfredo."

Edgar looked at his lover with discovered admiration. Why not indeed? You didn't *have* to do the same old things all the time, did you? "Coke and fries too?" he asked.

"You bet."

Edgar smiled, though Kelly could not see

it. "Don't let anyone take our table."

"Don't worry," she said. "I'll stake my life on it."

The line was short, so Edgar didn't have much time to reason. How could he eat a Big Mac and fries for breakfast? And a Coke? Really? He just couldn't.

The next thing he knew, he was staring at the young order taker, pert and bright eyed in her brown uniform.

"May I take your order, sir?"

"What?" he said, staring now at the board of options over her head. "Oh—yes, sorry...Two Big Macs, two fries, two Cokes."

Back at the table, Kelly said, "Ooo, good, you got the same—"

"Yeah, how could I not?"

"How indeed?" Kelly said, munching her hamburger.

"You know," he said, "fast food is really a miracle. Not cooked to order, cooked just ahead of the order. No waiting. Eat fast. Run. It could take all the pleasure out of eating—being too fast to give you time to think about it."

"Not me," Kelly said. "I like it just fine. Besides, it gives me more time to cuddle you."

"Yeah."

They savored their fast food in silence for a mere moment that stretched like a lifetime before them. Kelly broke it.

"You know," she said, "that maître d' was awful rude last night."

Edgar took a sip of Coke and nodded. "But I don't have any bad memories of last night," he said, "only good."

Kelly crinkled her eyes. "The good memories started later. I think that man should be taught a lesson."

Edgar's head bobbed in agreement. "How you gonna do that?"

"Let's think of something," she said, "we can't let him just get off scot-free. I wonder how many others he treats that way."

"But, so what are you going to do? We can't shoot him—"

"No—maybe—we could go in there and throw a pie in his face."

Edgar laughed.

"Saturday night. Rush hour, just go in and wham!" She pushed her palm forward to practice the motion. "What do you think would happen? I mean, would they arrest us do you think?"

"I don't know," he said. "Probably wouldn't want the fuss."

"Shall we do it?"

Edgar frowned. "Maybe there's something better. A pie in the face would be a momentary embarrassment. A couple people would see it happen—most of them would probably feel sorry for him. It should be something that cuts deeper—lasts longer."

"Like what?"

"Something that hurts him *and* the business. Something that relates to what he did to us. You know, making us wait all that time without giving us a table."

"Yeah," she said. "But what?"

They both took another chomp on their burgers.

"I got it," she said suddenly, setting the last corner of the Big Mac back in its cardboard home. "Let's book the whole restaurant for a Saturday night and not show up."

"Hah! Not bad. But do you think they'd do it? I mean, if we just called up and said, 'We want to book for Saturday the twelfth,' or something, he'd just say, 'Fine and dandy. We'll just close up and we'll see you then.' You can do that,

I expect, but only if you have big bucks and can prove it—in advance."

"So, we have a lot of people call. Reserve for two, four, six, whatever, until we've got the whole place. Use phony names."

Edgar smiled in admiration. "Not bad," he admitted.

"Not bad is right," she said. "Let's get right to it. I can have Bam call and Sheri, and a couple others. I'll call, you call. If we do it at different times and get different people, we won't even have to change our voices."

"Great!" he said.

"How far in advance should we do it? I mean, we don't want them suspicious all of a sudden they get booked up on a Saturday three months from now. But if we get too close to now it's liable to be half-booked already."

"So we call them and ask how far in advance they take reservations. Say we have a party of ten or twelve and are looking for a Saturday night. Then we go from there. I'd guess we'd want three, four weeks. They gave me our reservation less than a week before."

"Yeah, but it would be the best if we could get the whole place."

Kelly and Edgar

"You want to go back and see if we can peek through his log?" he asked. "It's usually right there on his podium."

"I think he'd recognize us. Maybe get suspicious. I say we call and ask how long in advance. If it's a long time, thank him and shoot for six weeks or so. If it's a short time, like only a month in advance, it's going to be tougher—but we take the last date."

"I'll call," he said.

When they got back to her apartment, he called. Saturday the twenty-eighth of next month was it. He asked for a table for eight.

"No problem."

Then they devoted themselves to more interpersonal warmth.

KELLY

"I'm in love, Bambi," I said. "Oh, I'm so in love."

"Went okay, did it?" Bambi asked as she came in the door from Sheri's place.

"It went sensational! God, I felt great. You were a dear to go to Sheri's. I owe you a big one."

"No biggie," Bambi said, opening the refrigerator door, then bending over, I guess in the hopes there was something on the bottom

Kelly

shelf more appealing than what she found at eye
level.

I was straddling the motorcycle and
watching Bambi's bottom enviously. She really
had sensational buns. I was so glad Eddie wasn't
here to see her rear.

"Is he leaving his wife?" Bambi asked the
bottom shelf.

"Well, I'm sure. But I'm not pushing that
so soon," I said. "I don't want to scare him away.
He's just the nicest man."

"They never do," Bambi said.

"Who never does what?"

"They never leave their wives."

"Oh, Bambi, you're such a downer," I
said. "I'm beginning to think you're jealous. I
mean—geez!"

I guess she didn't find anything appealing
on the bottom shelf either, because she stood up
and slammed the refrigerator door.

"Just realistic," she said.

But I knew she was a little jealous too.

I hopped off the motorcycle and grabbed
the state-of-the-art voice-activated telephone in
the main salon of our apartment. Then I threw a
leg back over the motorcycle saddle. Bambi sat at

the dinette table and leafed through a magazine.

"Hello," I said into the phone—"I'm calling for Michael Eisner of the Disney Studios. He'd like a table for six on Saturday the twenty-eighth of next month…yes…eight-thirty…good, thank you."

I hung up and turned to Bambi. "He didn't even ask for the phone number."

"What in the world are you doing?" Bambi asked, and I told her about our game.

Bambi had a good laugh. "Well, no wonder they didn't ask you for a phone number," Bambi said. "Not when you're calling for the richest guy in Hollywood."

"Yeah, that's one table there'll be no waiting for. Will you call tonight, Bam, when Snot-nose is on?"

"Yeah, sure. Who shall I say I am?"

"Let's go a nobody this time. But a hoity-toity-sounding name like William S. Churchill or something."

"And if they ask for a phone number?"

"Make one up—with a Beverly Hills prefix. This is the most fun I've had in ages."

"Hope it works," Bambi said.

"So do I."

PENELOPE

I think Edgar had his fling. Oh, he won't answer any questions about it, but a wife can tell. He doesn't bother to deny anything, he just gives me one of those looks that blames everything on me.

I came back from Denver to find him mooning around the house like a love-struck adolescent. At *his* age it is frankly disgusting.

That night I touched him in bed, just to get his reaction. I don't think I was asking for anything—I certainly didn't feel like it—but he pulled away. It was a sudden jerking motion, as though he had been propositioned by someone with leprosy.

So he makes believe he's asleep and I make believe I don't care. The next real conversation we have, I don't even remember when it was—the next day, the next week—he has the nerve to bring up divorce. What would I think? he wants to know. We never were all that compatible, he says. Imagine! This from old Straight-arrow himself. I always thought if there were any divorce broached in this household, I would do the broaching.

We didn't get anywhere with the subject because I don't see it serving any real purpose. What do I care if he has an affair? I could hardly care less. Wasn't I the one who told him to go ahead and have his fling? Do what he always wanted? And I do think I meant it. But maybe, deep down, I didn't expect he'd find the courage. What a nasty way to put it, courage! As though deceit required courage. Like equating infidelity with strength of character.

Of course, I've always said we make too much of sex. It really isn't that interesting—and other than being a perverse validation of a person's emotional worth in the eyes and libido of another person, the whole thing is vastly overrated. So I should care if Edgar finds a juvenile pleasure with a less cerebral woman? *Au contraire*.

Edgar didn't really have the luxury of a mid-life crisis—and now he's exiting the decade in which all the men in his family expired. He's got to feel the pressures of last-chanceitis.

And, if his room is any indication, he's feeling it bad. He has sketches and full-blown paintings of that bimbo everywhere. I feel sorry for him. Maybe it's time I admitted it may be *partially* my fault. We are what we are—and we want others to be not what *they* are, but what we *want* them to be. And I'm as guilty as the next person. But, men are animals. That's all there is to it.

Of course, sex is everywhere, in everything, and it isn't subtle anymore. It's blatant. Even on public television, you have it. I swear it won't be long before the churches find they can increase their attendance and membership being more explicit. Already they have singles groups, teenage get-togethers. You even hear about some groups having nude encounters.

So all these poor men get so pumped up

no one can satisfy them. Certainly these urges have to be built in or it would be the end of us. Not that that would bother *me* too much. I wasn't guilty of prolonging this mess. But the whole grand scheme of things is to keep it all going. I guess it would have to be or we wouldn't be here to talk about it. And it *is* fascinating. That's why I love the biological sciences.

Edgar is spending more time away from home now. He mumbles things like "Business trip," but he isn't fooling me. He's never been on a business trip in his life. Now he claims he's at a convention.

"What convention?" I ask.

"A book thing," he says.

I ask for the phone number of his hotel. He says he doesn't have it yet.

"Will you call me with it?"

He looks startled, then mutters about me not giving him my phone number when I go away.

"But you never ask for it," I protest, but he isn't paying any attention to me.

I made him a lot of food with beans and onions and garlic. Fart and halitosis food, but he wasn't interested in eating it. He wondered why I took such an interest in cooking all of a sudden.

It was a good idea but it didn't work. In desperation I ate it myself and I can tell you, it works. It caused me no small embarrassment at the university.

"Look here, Edgar," I said, "why don't you just tell me the truth? You don't have to sneak around here like a thief. You're having an affair, so okay. All I'm asking is to know where you are."

"Why?"

Why indeed? He had me there. If he were spending time with another woman (and what *else* would he be doing?), why would he want me to know where he was?

"In case something happens to you," I said lamely. "Or to me," I added.

He seemed on the verge of telling me something, perplexion crossed his face. Then he said:

"Call nine-one-one."

EDGAR AND KELLY

Edgar hung up the voice-activated state-of-the-art phone in Kelly's apartment and leaped off the floor.

He turned to slide his arm around Kelly's waist. Then, with both hands, lifted her from her perch on the motorcycle and vaulted her in the air.

"I'm sorry, sir," he said, mimicking his telephone correspondent, "we're completely booked."

"Yippee!" she shouted, and they danced beside the motorcycle and up the ladder to their own heaven to celebrate their considerable accomplishment.

Safe and snug in Edgar's arms, Kelly said, "Oh, Eddie, you are just the best lover in the whole world."

"No, you are."

"I don't ever want another lover as long as I live," she said, "because he could just never measure up."

"That's so nice of you, Kelly, but that could turn out to be a rash promise."

"Why? Are you going to leave me?"

"Not by choice—no. But we have to face it, I'm thirty-seven years ahead of you in the race. If we both live the same length of time, you'll be alone thirty-seven years. I wouldn't want you to suffer that. Not to mention that women still live longer than men."

"I'll have my memories," she said, "I'll live on those."

"Now, Kelly—"

"Or else I'll throw myself on the funeral fire like they do in India. I can't imagine going on without you. So you're just going to have to live a good long time."

He shook his head. "For the first time, I have something to live for. If it was just you and me, I'd want to live forever."

"Who else is there?" she asked.

"Not who, how. My family isn't known for male longevity."

"Then you're going to have to be the first."

"Fine with me," he said.

"Eddie, what did I tell you about this downer talk?"

"Yes, yes, I'm sorry."

"You're probably going to outlive me anyway."

"That would be a tragedy. You are so blissfully loving, so startlingly sensual, you should be the eternal love goddess."

"You're sweet, Eddie," she said.

They stayed in each other's arms in the loft as they had before, until they were weak from hunger.

"Eat?" he said.

They agreed they couldn't go back to McDonald's this time. So he took her to the Hamburger Hamlet he had stopped at after he had met her.

There in a booth in the semi-darkness, with the Shakespeare memorabilia all around, they plotted the denouement of their Pierre Francois strategy. They reviewed the reservations they had made and the phone numbers they left.

"I'll be at my number to verify that our table for eight is still coming. You'll be at yours. We said we'd be out all day on about sixteen. Gave phony numbers on the rest. Let's hope some are no-answers and disconnects."

"Or they don't call until they don't show," he said.

"Cross your fingers," she said and crossed hers.

She had the hamburger with the blue cheese and bacon. "I'm going to blow up like a balloon," she said.

He repeated his onion soup from the day they met. "A nostalgic choice," he apologized when she cast a puzzled glance at him. He explained, "I'm trying to let some more air out of this balloon."

"Eddie, you're perfect," she said, and he was overwhelmed because she actually seemed to believe it.

The Real Sleeper

While they waited for the food, Edgar noticed he was getting a sore throat. He swallowed several times, drank two glasses of water.

"Is something wrong?" Kelly asked.

"Just feels like I might be getting a little sore throat. You have one?"

"No," she said, "but I don't care if I get it. If you have it, I want it."

*　　　*　　　*

Two weeks flew by. Edgar had taken two long weekends—told Penelope he was going to publishing conferences and realized she didn't believe him. He didn't know why he cared what she thought, but apparently he did, because he kept trying to deceive her, without any real success.

During the week, Edgar went through the motions at work, reading manuscripts and doing rudimentary editing, and falling asleep in the afternoons to catch up.

Kelly went out on interviews and a few readings. She got only one modeling job in the two weeks, and decided it was because she was haggard—with good reason.

Bambi had been a most obliging roommate. She went to visit her family in Missouri for one of the trysts and spent the other with Sheri. She had given up nagging Kelly about Edgar's wife.

Edgar had thought on one of his trips back to Thousand Oaks that he might begin to tire of Kelly—or more likely, she might soon begin to tire of him. After all, they were *so different*—how could they be *more* different? he wondered. He liked to be with her all right, but the one thing they had so strongly in common was an insatiable sexual attraction.

When would it become satiable? Edgar asked Kelly that Sunday afternoon.

"Never in the world," she responded, wrapping her legs around him and kissing everything she could reach.

"Oh, God," he said, "I hope you're right."

"I'm right," she said.

"Mmmmmm."

"Eddie," she said, propping herself up on an elbow.

"Hm?"

"You know what I'd like to do?"

"Hm?"

"I'd like to read some of the really good books so I could talk to you about them. Could you give me a list? Start with some pretty easy ones first. You know I'm not a genius."

Edgar smiled. He retrieved a pen from the pocket of his pants, which were jumbled on the floor. "Paper?"

She hopped out of bed and rummaged around her small dresser. Edgar watched the sensuous movements of her naked back—sinuous, soft, slinking—until she located a tablet she used for grocery lists. She bounced back on the bed and gave Edgar a kiss on the cheek as she handed the tablet to him.

"You know you don't have to do this for me," he said. "I love you just as you are. I couldn't love you any more if you were the world's biggest genius."

"Well, there's a fat chance of *that*," she said.

Naked in bed, Edgar began making the list. He started with *Catcher in the Rye*, always a beloved beginning. Then added *Huckleberry Finn*. He made a second column, headed "For Later," and put under the heading *Moby Dick*; *An American Tragedy*; *Sister Carrie*; *Billy Budd*,

Foretopman; and *U.S.A.*

In the first column, he added *Alice in Wonderland; Babbitt; All the King's Men; Gone With the Wind; A Separate Peace;* and *Lord of the Flies.*

"How many do you want?"

"A thousand," she said, jumping up eagerly to lift the list. "A good start," she said approvingly. "Any love stories?" she asked sheepishly.

"Sure. *Gone With the Wind.* They're all about love of one sort or another," he said.

"How about our kind of love?"

He frowned. "Maybe the Europeans—*Bovary, Karenina,* but these first. *American Tragedy* is a powerful love story. But it doesn't have a happy ending. Not much of it is happy really, and the writing isn't as smooth as we might like, but it's a powerful story. Of course, the guy is young, and he is taking advantage of the girl."

"What about us? Isn't there one about us?"

Edgar thought for a moment, rubbing the top of the pen across his lips. Then he smiled and in block letters added to his list, *LOLITA.*

"*Lolita,*" she exclaimed, looking at the tablet. "Isn't that about a child and a dirty old man?"

"Well?"

"Oh, Eddie, you're funneee," she said. "Well, I guess I got my work cut out for me. I better get a library card."

"I'll loan you some to start."

"No, you shouldn't have to do that. I have to show some gumption here. Besides, if I get them at the library, I'll feel compelled to read them in two weeks. It'll be another incentive."

"Okay," he said. "But if you can't find any of them, I have most of them and I'd be so happy to have you read any of mine."

"You're sweet," she said, and kissed his nose. "Eddie?"

"Hm?"

"I don't want you to go back to Thousand Oaks."

"Yeah, I don't want to either."

"Then stay here."

"What would Bambi do?"

"She has her own space—we won't bother each other."

Edgar raised an eyebrow.

"She's had men staying here before."

"How long?"

"Well, a couple days."

Edgar didn't say anything. He was thinking.

"We could try it," Kelly offered.

"You know what I want to do?" Edgar asked.

"What?"

"Take you sports-car shopping."

"Oh, Eddie, you don't want…"

"No, really."

"Looks to me like you already won my heart, without having to give me any old car keys."

"I just feel like I want to give you everything you want."

"Well, all's I want is you, Eddie."

Edgar frowned. "Honest?" he asked.

"Honest," she said.

He frowned some more.

"What's amatter, lover?" Kelly asked.

"Nothing," he said. "I just can't believe I could be so lucky."

"Well, believe it," she said. "Nobody's going to stop me believing my luck."

"Kelly?"

"Yes, love?"

"Would you let me get you a place in

The Real Sleeper

Santa Barbara?"

"Well, you mean an apartment or something?"

"Yeah."

"Why, sure, I *would.*"

"You would?"

"You bet."

"But what about your work?"

"I'd just drive down when I need to. They have telephones in Santa Barbara, don't they?"

His smile swallowed his face, and his hug flattened her breasts between them.

The Sunday-night departure was put off until Monday morning. He would stop at home on his way in to work. And that night they experienced a more frantic closeness and even more satisfying bonding than ever.

When he kissed her goodbye that Monday morning, they had a discussion on how much sleep they had gotten. She said four hours, he thought two at the most.

Driving home, he felt his age for the first time since he began loving Kelly. His throat was sore, he had a headache and he was bone weary. Perhaps he should call the office and tell them he was sick. He could go to bed and see if he felt better around noon. Lord, he was two months from sixty and this lack of sleep had to be taking its toll.

Can't let myself get so run down, he thought. Not when I have, at last, something to live for.

*   *   *

On Saturday the twenty-eighth, Kelly and Edgar spent the day together in the loft. He had meant to be home to answer his phone in case the restaurant called, but he just couldn't stay away from her. Edgar still had his sore throat and he was surprised at Kelly's indifference to it. Did she really want to catch it? he wondered.

Well, he thought, a guy who has been as repressed as long as I have shouldn't look a gift horse in the mouth. Sore throats go away. There are a lot worse things.

And so they loved, as another Edgar once said, "with a love that was more than love."

They talked about the books she had already read: *Catcher in the Rye*—"That's just the neatest book," she said; and *Gone With the Wind*— "That Scarlett, I *swear*. And I started *All the King's Men*. That's harder going, but I think I'll like it."

They were as nervous as schoolkids as they prepared for their evening outing to Pierre Francois. Kelly kept asking Edgar if she looked all right, if this matched that, if she had on too much lipstick. He reassured her she looked smashing.

"Not too sexy?" she asked.

"There is no such thing," he said, taking her in his arms.

The voice-activated state-of-the-art phone rang. Kelly answered the extension upstairs. "Yes, it is," she said, looking at Edgar smiling broadly. "That's right, eight at eight-thirty. We'll be there."

She dropped the phone with a flourish of flying hands. "Whooee!" she said, "I think it's gonna work."

They had started their reservations at seven and they had no idea how many others had been able to slip into the cracks, and they were so anxious to find out that they drove to the posh eatery at ten minutes before seven. The parking lot was empty except for the extra personnel Saturday-night crew of four valet parkers in maroon vests standing in a group.

Edgar and Kelly

"Oh, look," Kelly said, clapping her hands, "they're just hanging out, rapping. Oh, Eddie, I think it worked."

"Little soon to tell, maybe," he said. "Early for a Saturday night."

He nosed the Ford onto Wilshire, then headed up La Cienega to Sunset. Restaurant Row was bustling, Kelly pointed out.

"But Pierre Francois is a tonier place. The *haut monde* dines later," Edgar cautioned.

They cruised Sunset Boulevard, then up to Hollywood Boulevard, but the freak show was not yet in full stride. There being only assorted transvestites, pimps and hookers roaming listlessly as though biding their time before the big show started.

They returned to Beverly Hills via La Cienega's restaurant row again. The row was jumping: cars pulling in, valet parkers hopping, a stream of expectant diners pouring into the restaurants.

Here were restaurants mom and pop could go to when they shot their wad and drove from back home in Iowa or Arkansas or wherever it was. Like as not, they would get a smile from a hostess, a smile that didn't put her out all that much and yet carried enough zest to make them feel welcome, if not exactly at home.

When Kelly and Edgar turned onto the street off Wilshire where Pierre Francois was located they could feel the vacuum and it thrilled them to the quick. The valet-parking boys were still standing around, the lot was still empty.

Inside they were greeted by Jacques, the venerable maître d'. "Good evening," he said, his casing of the May-to-December couple somewhat less judgmental than at their last visit.

"Two," Edgar said with a simple presumption that Kelly would later tell him was so fabulous.

"Do you have a reservation, sir?" Jacques said with *gravitas*, examining his overfull schedule.

"I'm afraid not."

"Oh, sir," Jacques said with maximum disappointment, "I'm afraid we are completely booked."

Without saying anything, Edgar made exaggerated gestures of surveying the empty place. He looked at the maître d' and said, "Really?" Then he looked at his watch. "What time are they getting here?"

"Yes," Jacques admitted, "some of them are quite late."

Edgar looked at the numerous names on the list. "I see, you are heavily booked. Oh, look—Eisner for six—is that Michael Eisner?"

"Yes, it is, sir." The major-domo did not disguise his pride. That would have been tacky.

"Gee, I'd like to meet *him*!" Kelly said.

"I'm afraid we could not allow any intrusion into our patrons' privacy."

"Well, they sure could have a lot of privacy here tonight," Kelly said with an engaging down-home wonder.

"So you can't seat us?" Edgar pressed.

Jacques frowned and consulted his list, then scanned his empty dining room.

"Maybe we should wait for a cancellation," Kelly said.

"Nah," Edgar disagreed, "let's go someplace else. They're completely booked."

"But I don't see anybody." Kelly was playing the bumpkin.

"They'll be pouring in any minute," Edgar said. "We'd just better go on before we get stampeded."

The Real Sleeper

Jacques was frowning. It seemed to Edgar that he had foolishly committed himself to the full-house scenario but was having some serious second thoughts.

"If you would wait a minute here, sir, let me check something with the kitchen." And he disappeared into the dining room.

"What do you suppose he's looking for?" Kelly asked.

"I suppose he's milking the situation for a tip."

"Well, don't you give him one."

"Don't worry."

Jacques returned. "I think I will be able to seat you now, sir." He picked a couple of over-sized menus out of their bin and led the parade into the dining room to a table at the far end.

"Aren't we lucky," Kelly cooed, and Edgar saw no reason she shouldn't get any acting part she went for.

"Your waiter will be with you in a moment," Jacques said. And so he was—a tall guy, every bit as imperial looking as the major-domo.

"Not too much business tonight," Edgar observed to the waiter.

"No, sir, it is very strange. We were completely booked."

"Is that so?"

He nodded gravely. "We are used to no-shows. It is part of the business, but we allow for that and usually on Saturday it is standing room only."

"You overbook, like the airlines?" Edgar asked.

"Not so much, no, sir, but there is some leeway."

"So I guess sometimes you could have a reservation and not get a table."

His eyebrows went up. "It happens, sir. We would always serve a customer. However, the wait can be quite long."

"I suppose you make allowances for celebrities."

"Well, of course. Michael Eisner reserved for tonight."

"Oh, really?" Edgar asked. "Where is he?" He craned his neck at the empty tables.

The waiter shrugged his shoulders. "He is among the no-shows."

"Well, I guess we are lucky then. We didn't even *have* a reservation."

"Oh, sir, very lucky indeed. On a Saturday night it is not possible to dine at Pierre Francois without a reservation."

"Except tonight," Kelly chimed in.

"Yes, ma'am," the waiter admitted, dropping his head at the shame of it all. "Are you ready to order?"

"Oh, yes," Kelly chirped, "I'll try the house salad."

"Very good, madame, and for your entrée?"

"Oh, just the salad."

He hoisted an eyebrow.

"On a diet," she explained.

"And you, sir?"

"Oh, I'll just share her salad."

The waiter's demeanor slipped from being the friend and confidant to a wary, if circumspect, adversary.

"Perhaps a nice Caesar salad for two?" he offered. "Prepared at the table."

Edgar screwed up his face as though he were giving it some thought. "No, thanks," he finally decided.

The waiter swallowed his disgust, but not without letting his customers taste the full force of it. He was, after all, the senior waiter in the shop. That was why he had been given this first table for the evening.

"And your entrée, sir?" He pronounced it with more hope than confidence.

"Oh, I'll just see how the salad is. If it's good, I'll order something else."

"Very good, sir," the waiter said in that understated tone of disdain, and he retreated to the kitchen with a gait and bearing of heavy disappointment.

Edgar covered his giggle with a sip of water. Kelly covered hers with the back of her hand.

"What do you bet we never see the salad?" Kelly asked Edgar.

"It's a good bet," Edgar said, "but I think we will. They must have an awful lot of lettuce back there, and a place like this wouldn't deign to serve day-old lettuce."

"Oh, Edgar, surely lettuce will last more than a day."

"Maybe—but you got to admit they are probably in the mood to move a little lettuce tonight."

"Yeah," she said, "not to mention the frog legs."

While they waited, the maître d' sauntered over to their table.

"Oh, oh, here he comes," Kelly warned.

"Is everything all right?" he asked.

"So far," Edgar said. "Of course, all we've had was the bread and water—but that's just fine."

"Oh." The maître d' looked crestfallen. "He did not take your drink order? I'm sorry."

"Oh, no," Edgar assured him, "we don't drink. We're just waiting for the food."

"Very good, sir, and if it is not too late, might I recommend the Châteaubriand for two?" He looked pointedly at Kelly and said, "It is a very romantic dish."

"We'll keep that in mind," Edgar said, "thanks."

Edgar was right: the salad came amid servisorial fanfare. When it was set in front of the loving couple and they had a chance to focus on it, their eyes flashed with a mixture of astonishment and I-told-you-so.

On the gold-rimmed plate, which seemed the size of a Little League baseball diamond, sat a sphere of lettuce the size of a softball. Kelly and Edgar stared at the mixture of greens, then at the smug waiter, then at each other, then at the empty plate that was being ceremoniously slid into the empty space before Edgar. The waiters (two) took two steps back and bowed, which Edgar thought could have been part of the routine, or could have been simply a formal gesture of ridicule, but he didn't care. As soon as the wait staff retreated with a crisp, if somewhat derisive, "*Bon appétit*," Kelly served Edgar a few leaves of the delicate greenery.

Wishing to prolong their stay at the table with a minimum investment, Kelly and Edgar savored one leaf at a time, giving each an eternity of mastication, in an effort to revel in the agony of the house.

As they were grinding down on the last leaf, they spied the maître d' marching toward them. His gait struck Edgar as a mixture of a macho Italian mating stride and a Gestapo march, with one arm swinging more than the other.

"How was your salad, sir?"

Edgar eyed him silently for a moment, reaching for the appropriate insult. "Good of you to ask. A little oily for my taste," he said, and turned to Kelly for her opinion. "You?"

"Oily." She nodded. "Definitely, oily."

"And some of the lettuce wasn't quite as crisp as I might have hoped," Edgar said.

"Really, sir?" The maître d's eyebrows were in the high-five position.

"Soggy." Kelly nodded.

"Are you quite sure the leaves were fresh?" Edgar asked.

"Well, of course," the maître d' took, as they say, umbrage.

"_Very_ soggy," Kelly added.

"Well, I am sorry, sir. If you had only told us, we would have been glad to bring you a substitute."

"Thanks, but my mother always told me, 'Accept no substitutes.'"

"If you will try the Châteaubriand," the maître d' offered, recovering some composure, "I guarantee you will not be disappointed."

Edgar looked at Kelly. "What do you say, dear?"

"I frankly didn't think the salad showed much class, and if it's beef you want, McDonald's is still open."

Edgar looked up at the maître d' and spread his hands in a gesture of hopelessness. He rose and deposited his napkin on his empty salad plate. Kelly followed suit.

"But, sir..." The maître d' was working up to revealing some anger. "Where do you think...?"

"You heard the lady. I'm afraid the place regrettably just doesn't measure up to our taste." Edgar paused to wave a hand about the room. "I suppose I should have guessed anyplace empty on a Saturday night must have serious problems."

Kelly had taken Edgar's arm and they had started out of the room when, hoping to avert a complete loss, the maître d' said, "Wait, I'll get you your bill, sir."

"No need," Edgar said. "We wouldn't pay it anyway. Just comp the whole thing."

"And be sure and add a generous tip for the waiters and yourself," Kelly added with a blithe, yet proprietorial wave of her left hand.

"But you can't..." the major-domo of the establishment was sputtering. The couple didn't wait to hear the rest of his protest.

In the parking lot they found their car parked next to a Rolls-Royce right by the door.

The attendant knew which car to bring. No less than three valets attended to them as the

The Real Sleeper

car rolled up. The driver bounced out as another held his door open, and the third opened the passenger door for Kelly.

The attendant holding the door asked, "Did you have a nice evening, sir?"

"Very gratifying," Edgar said, "thank you." And he laid a five-dollar tip in the hand of the driver, while three other valet soldiers paid them homage.

"Oh, thank you, sir." The gratitude was heartfelt.

"Say, whose Rolls is this?" Edgar asked the lad. "I didn't see anyone else in there."

He gave an embarrassed laugh. "It's the owner's. We park it here all the time. Gives the place class, I guess," he said.

"Class?" Kelly spoke up. "I didn't see any sign of it inside, did you, dear?"

Edgar frowned. "No," he said, "come to think of it, don't believe I did. All the class tonight is in the parking lot."

The boys grinned, and Edgar drove off with Kelly beside him. After he turned right at the first corner, Edgar had to pull over to the curb. They were both laughing so hard their sides hurt.

PENELOPE

This ridiculous business with Edgar was starting to bother more than I care to admit. I'd come to the point where I was considering psychiatry when I thought of Janice Easton, my colleague at the university.

Janice is a with-it, hip professor of psychology and even had a brief stint teaching a dumbing-down course they call Marriage and the Family. Did her doctoral on the biological basis for the psychological differences between men and women, something like that—a little narrower, of course, with a more esoteric title.

And Janice was not devoid of practical experience, having tripped to the altar herself multiple times. Of course, I'd no idea what I must have been thinking. What did I expect from a veteran of the multi-marriage scene? Roses?

I took her to lunch at the Faculty Club. I got there first and took a table on the edge of the bright room, where we might enjoy a modicum of privacy. I liked the club. It wasn't a "club" really, just another one of those labels calculated to make us lowly teachers feel important. It was a utilitarian dining room: neat, clean and pedestrian, but someone brought you your food, so it was a cut above the student cafeteria.

I am ashamed to say I didn't realize until I saw her coming at me that I hadn't seen her for too long. Not since her last divorce. She was wearing this mannish gray suit with an almost-necktie kind of red cloth hanging in front. She must have put on twenty-five pounds or so, but she still had that _joie-de-vivre_ bounce in her step.

For some reason her outfit intimidated me and I felt self-conscious about my black dress.

But, I *was* in mourning.

"You're looking wonderful, darling," she said, leaning over for a hug. "You just never age."

I had to say something. What do *you* say? "Your skin, I swear, it gets younger every time I see you."

She sat and laughed. "That's the upside of fat. It stretches your skin—smooths out the wrinkles."

We did the small-talk bit: "It's been too long"—"How long's it been?"—"What's happening in your life?"—the whole routine.

We ordered. I asked for a salad with a slice of lemon, and Janice's eyes shot up. She ordered the roast-beef sandwich. "I just *love* beef," she defended her choice, "and I just get so fed up with everyone bad-mouthing it. But you aren't sick, are you?"

"No, why?"

"Lettuce and lemon?"

I did feel a little foolish. I was thinner than she was and I was playing the anorexic.

"I mean, *lettuce*? We call it God's revenge."

I tried to wave off her concern with my hand. "Just trying to be a little more desirable to my man," I explained.

"Yeah?" She was surprised. "You got a boyfriend?"

"No—my *husband*."

"Oh—really? Edgar you mean? Really?"

I nodded.

"But...why?"

"He's found himself a twenty-three-year-old."

"No? Edgar? Really?"

"Yes, Edgar," I said, and poured out the story.

Janice listened like a good pal.

"I don't think you ever understood men, Penelope," she said. "Or perhaps you understood them *too* well. In the practical world there is such a thing as being too bright for your own good. If the game is stupid you refuse to play it. Most of us play the game on our own terms. You can't run away from that built-in itch the poor suckers have. Not and preserve your marriage. You seem to have gotten away with it longer than most. So why do you want to preserve it?"

I didn't know what to say to her.

"It's ego, isn't it? Hey, you don't have to try to fool me, I've had three of them. Each divorce came easier, till finally I woke up and said, 'Hey, what are you trying to prove? That you can find a man somewhere you can get along with? Or maybe a man who can get along with you? One you can please at the same time vice versa—and not demean yourself in the process?' You know what it is? It's a convention, is all. Why do these blue-haired ladies make such fools out of themselves in pursuit of some old fart? What is she buying but a potful of headaches and a patient to nurse to his bitter end? And contrary to popular belief, old people don't get mellow unless they're out of it. They get nasty."

The food was served.

"So why?" I asked, looking for a lettuce leaf to spear.

"Convention. They've lived a life where the women with hubbies were considered the successful ones—the lucky ones. Families. There's nothing like a picture of a mom and dad and a couple of kids to get the tear ducts working. And hey, I'm not going to knock it. If you have any hope of keeping civilization on its feet, you've got to get the boys and girls together. And girls want boys for babies, and boys want girls for fun, fair enough. But after you've done your duty and the fertilizing factory shuts down, what on earth is the point of prolonging the agony? It's *over*, girls. What you came for is *accomplished*. You are ful*filled*. Where is it written you have to suffer for the rest of your life because you used some jerk to pump a little seed for the species?"

"But I never had a child," I said.

"All the more reason. What do you want with him?"

"I don't know. Companionship? Someone to talk to."

"Does he listen?"

"I don't know. Not much, I guess."

"Do *you* listen?"

"Not much."

"Face it. Are you more comfortable talking to him or to me?"

"Well...to you right now."

"Exactly what I discovered. That's the main reason my next husband is going to be a woman."

"Janice!"

"So—you're shocked? I can't tell you what a relief it is to be out of the man scene. My father would always say I could do better after he met some guy I brought home. Now I see he was right. Where is there a man good enough for _any_ woman?"

"Wow," I said, poking at my salad. "I'm glad I came to you for advice."

"Oh, you didn't need me. You could have figured it out if you put your mind to it."

"But your outlook is so dreary."

"I'm just looking at what's there. And I'm not alone. Look at the kids today. They don't get married anymore. They just live together. It's being married without having to _be_ married. Serial monogamy. Even girls and guys who _do_ get married had several spouses before the first government-sanctioned hitching. You know the old saying: Why buy the cow when the milk is free?"

"Okay, Janice—you're wearing me out. I guess your advice is clear—get out fast—dump him."

"The sooner the better," she said.

Sorry I asked her. I guess in the final analysis I'm no better than anyone else. When I seek advice, I am seeking a validation of my pre-conceived biases. What I wanted her to say was: "By God, you stand on your hind legs and roar, 'I'm not giving up _my_ man!'"

Janice really turned into a depressant.

"But don't you think he might outgrow it?"

"Sure, and then what? Life could just outgrow him at the same time. Just in time for you to gear up for your nursing stint."

"Hey, Janice, he's not that old."

"Well, he must be pretty far gone; this smacks of one of those last-chance flings."

"Okay, okay. I guess you have no use at all for men anymore—but once you were pretty adroit at getting them. How did you do it?"

"Really, Penelope? I can't believe you are asking me this. You are what, fifty-some? and you're asking a kindergarten biology question? You can't be serious."

I nodded solemnly.

"You've never done anything..like...sexy?"

I shook my head, but I realized that was an exaggeration. Anyway, I wanted to hear what *she* had to say.

"So do something sexy." She shrugged.

"Like what?"

"Like something he likes."

"What?"

"Come on, Penelope, if you seriously

don't know what he likes, or even if you think I know better, you ought to just bow out. Check out the gay scene. Who knows what women want more than another woman?"

I shook my head. I didn't know much, but I knew I didn't want *that*!

Janice seemed to really look at me for the first time. She reached across the table and took my hands in hers. "Oh, honey," she said, "don't tell me deep down you really love him?"

"I don't know," I said. I was confused. "I'm *used* to him. He's like—family."

"But surely you realize men are just children? The older they get, the more childlike they become. You know how many of them are absolute babies before they die. Do you really want a baby on your hands?"

"I...well...I don't..." I was not doing a good job of expressing myself. I'm sure Janice wondered how I could ever maintain order and teach anything in a classroom. "I guess I must want to keep him...for some reason. He's a good enough person—better than nothing," I stumbled around the topic. "Could I do better now? I don't want to."

"Then go for it," Janice said, releasing my hands.

I felt a lot better as I unconsciously slid my hands in my lap.

"How?"

"Come on, we're dealing with a baby. Edgar? I've met Edgar. He's a lamb. Babies thrive on creature comforts. He needs to be fed and loved. That's all. Soon he'll need to be changed too, but you can cross that bridge when you come to it."

"Yes, I can feed him, but he's less and less interested in food. It's the love part..." I trailed off in uncertainty and embarrassment.

"LOVE!" she shouted so the whole room looked at us, I swear. "We aren't talking *love*, we're talking screwing!"

Janice was so crude sometimes. Forthright would be a nicer way to put it, but then, isn't that why I turned to her in the first place? I dropped my eyelids like a coy debutante.

"Janice," I muttered, not looking at her, hoping the eyes of the room were finally off us, "I never was too good at that. Now he's found a twenty-three-year-old sexpot. How in the world could I ever compete with that?"

Janice snickered. The wad of roast beef she was chewing didn't slow her down. "That reminds me of a story," she said. "There was this old guy, about Edgar's age, I'd say, who had been married several times, I guess. Anyway, his wife was twenty and gorgeous; he was sixty. Lo and behold, it was discovered he had a sixty-five-year-old mistress. So somebody asked him, 'My God, what has this old mistress got that your beautiful young wife doesn't?' His answer? 'Patience.'"

I laughed.

She shrugged. "So try it if you want. Personally, I'd cut him loose."

"I don't know what it is, Janice. Listening to you it all sounds so trite. But maybe there is a comfort in continuity. Permanence. Especially at our time of life."

She shrugged again. "Then you have to work at it," she said.

"That's my problem," I said. "I don't ever feel like it."

She nodded as though I were hopeless. "Feel like it," she advised. "Or he isn't going to feel like sticking around. In marriage, you know, if you want it to stick, you have to give more than you get. Both of you. And still you'll be doing precious little for your mate. Everybody thinks they are giving about seventy percent when each is really giving about twelve."

She had the cheesecake for dessert and I had a cup of tea—no sugar. We promised to do this more often, but I got the queasy feeling she was looking at me the way men do sometimes.

On the sidewalk, we hugged goodbye, but I was lackluster.

"First lesson," she said, "put more squeeze in your hug," and she was bouncing toward Psychology, while I turned toward Zoology.

Back at my desk in my cluttered office I thought about Edgar and the advice Janice had given me. I can't say she didn't make a lot of sense, but I just knew I was not cut out to stomach the lesbian scene.

Instead I would rear up on my hind legs and bay at the moon. I wasn't about to let a twenty-three-year-old bimbo hog my territory. Thirty-five years had to count for something. I wouldn't let him go—not without a fight. He's *mine*!

KELLY AND EDGAR

Edgar had left work an hour and a half early to help Kelly christen the apartment he'd rented for her in Santa Barbara.

They were in bed, but this strenuous life that would have taxed a teenager was taking its toll on Edgar. He was running out of steam, he told Kelly.

"That's all right, Eddie. I just love to be near you—the nearer the better. You don't have to do anything at all."

It was a cozy little one-room place on the second floor of a sixty-year-old building within striking distance of the ocean. The walls were off-white and the carpet was beige and the bed pulled out of the wall. But there was a full kitchen in back. It wasn't modern or anything like it, but everything worked, and Kelly was in heaven having her own place.

There were books on the table, books on the couch, books on the floor. Kelly was using all her free time in a frantic effort to catch up with Edgar's lifetime of reading.

The sun shone in in the late afternoon, but was mercifully nowhere to be seen in the early morning, so Kelly could sleep in if she didn't have to go to L.A. for interviews or a shoot. But she didn't sleep as much as she used to. She got up to read. *Madame Bovary* currently; *Billy Budd* just finished.

Edgar sat up in bed and felt a sudden pounding in his head. Kelly pulled him back down. "Hey, where do you think you're goin'?"

"I think, for your sake and mine, not to mention your bed, I should go to the bathroom."

When he came back he sat on the bed

and she pulled him over. "Oh, Eddie, I love you so much. This is just the nicest apartment you got me, Eddie. Oooo, I'm *so* happy here," Kelly said. "You don't have any smog and the weather's so nice. And to be close to you—I just never felt better. You know what I wish?"

"What?"

"I could be with you always. Like I could go and spend the day in your desk drawer at work—I wouldn't say anything to, you know, bother you, but I'd just be there with you."

"That would be nice," he said. "But I'd have to get an awful big desk, or you'd have to shrink."

Kelly laughed.

"Do you want to have some dinner with me?" he asked, "or shall I leave you now?"

"Oh, Eddie. Don't *ever* leave me."

"Well, just for the night."

"I don't want you to go—even for the night."

"So let's get dinner." He got out of bed, and Kelly, pouting her displeasure, followed.

"Where do you want to go?" he asked.

"You know what we never did?"

"What?"

"We never went for sushi."

"Yeah. Want to?"

"Let's."

They drove to the little sushi bar in Victoria Court and sat at a tiny table, one of a half-dozen in the place.

"You order for me, will you?" Edgar asked. "You're the sushi buff."

She was pleased at his confidence, and she ordered with a quiet authority that made him proud.

When the waitress headed back to the counter, Edgar asked Kelly, "How did Bambi take your moving?"

"She was a pretty good sport. I said I'd pay till she got someone, but Sheri moved right in."

"That was lucky."

"Yeah," Kelly said, then frowned. "You know, Eddie, Bambi's been on me from the beginning about your wife."

"Oh?" he said. "Not much her affair, would you say?"

"N-n-oo. I guess she's got my interests at heart though."

"What did you tell her?"

"That you were the most wonderful man

in the world and I had perfect trust in you to do the right thing. I said if you had four hundred wives I'd still love you, want you, give my life for you."

"You know what, sweetie?" Edgar asked.

"Hm?"

"I'm pooped."

"Well, I should say. We've been staying up all night for how long?"

"Who counts?"

"Yeah."

"Would you mind if I went back home tonight?"

"Oh, Eddie—why?"

"To sleep," he laughed.

"I'll let you sleep, I promise. I'll stay in the kitchen if you want."

"Yeah, but I can't do it. When I'm next to you in bed, sleep seems an anachronism."

"A which?"

"A something out of step. Something I can't do."

"So you want to go back to your mean old wife so she can bore you to sleep?"

Edgar smiled. "I guess you put your finger on it," he said. "But only for tonight. I'll be back tomorrow. We'll have lunch on the beach."

"Really? All RIGHT!" she said. "Well, if you must. I haven't had so much sleep either. I used to be this big sleeper—before I met you."

"I remember."

"Oh, how would you know?"

"You told me, at the shoot."

"I did?"

Edgar nodded. "You said you had no social life so you went to bed at seven and sometimes didn't get up till noon."

"Really?"

"Wasn't it true?"

"Sure it was. I just am surprised I told a perfect stranger that," Kelly said. "I must have trusted you from the moment I laid eyes on you."

The raw fish arrived, arranged so artistically on the large plate, interspersed with green-rimmed sushi. Kelly dug in with gusto; Edgar went at it more gingerly, not being a dyed-in-the-wool sushi aficionado.

"So what are you reading, Eddie?" she asked.

"Wow," he said, "I never thought I wouldn't have an answer to that question. You've zapped all my time and energy. I can hardly keep my eyes open at work, let alone read." Then he added, sheepishly, "You?"

"I just finished *Billy Budd*," she said. "What do you make of it, Eddie? It's a real sadness, isn't it?"

"Yes."

"I mean, I don't understand why Captain Vere didn't just kick that awful man out of the navy—that Claggart—instead of having poor Billy killed. I mean, do you?"

"Some say it's an allegory of good and evil."

"What's an allegory?"

"It's talking about something when you mean it to represent something else. Like a metaphor. You know what a metaphor is..."

She shook her head. "I wasn't very good in school. I didn't pay much attention..." she apologized.

"A metaphor is, oh, the sun shone like melted butter. That means the sun could remind you of melted butter, though, of course, it isn't butter. It is a way of saying something that puts you in mind of something else. They fought like cats and dogs—they aren't cats or dogs but people; cats and dogs fight with each other, so you know it was a scrappy fight."

"So what's that got to do with _Billy Budd_?"

"It is a simple story of good and evil. Claggart is a nasty piece of work. Billy is simple goodness personified. Claggart can't abide Billy's almost naive goodness. His popularity for his guilelessness. So Claggart provokes him until Billy hits him. And Claggart dies.

"In those days, that meant death. Captain Vere was a good man, but his hands were tied—another metaphor—and he had to order the death of an innocent man in order to _keep_ order on the ship. Evil provokes good. Good kills evil. Good executes good."

"You mean it's like nice guys don't win ball games?" she asked.

"I don't think that's..."

"Or, the good die young?"

"That might be more like it. But maybe it's more subtle. There is good in the world, but it is often innocent—and evil often vanquishes good. Innocence is easy prey for evil."

"Yeah," she said, "and it shouldn't be."

"And that's how you feel after you read Melville's allegory. So the author did his job."

Edgar put his hand to his throat and massaged it with his fingers.

"How *is* your throat?"

Edgar cleared it. "Still sore."

"Not getting better?"

He shook his head.

"Maybe you should see a doctor."

"I'm not much for doctors," he said. "Colds, sore throats, sinus, all pretty normal. They just sell you a bunch of pills that lower your resistance for the next time."

"Yeah, well, you don't have to *take* the pills—just see what he says."

"She."

"What?"

"What *she* says. My doctor's a woman."

"Oh, wow, Eddie, should I be jealous?"

He fixed her with an eternal gaze. "You will never have to be jealous," he said, "as long as I live."

"Oh, Eddie, I just had this most terrible thought."

"No bad thoughts, remember?" Edgar said. "What is it?" he asked when she seemed to turn inward.

"I just had this most terrible premonition

The Real Sleeper

that if you went away from me tonight I'd never see you again."

"Oh, Kelly, you are the best thing that ever happened to me. When I'm away from you I think about you all the time."

"Even when you're with your wife?"

"Now, Kelly, you know better."

"So why are you going back to her?"

"I'm *not* going *back* to her, Kelly. I'm simply taking a breather. Most of my clothes are still there."

"Why don't you bring your clothes to my place?"

"I will," he said.

"Really?" Her eyes opened with hope.

"Are you going to talk about a divorce?"

Edgar stared at Kelly for a long time. "You know, I have...a little," he said.

But Kelly didn't believe it.

When he took her back to the apartment, she asked him to come in "for just a minute." He protested he wouldn't get out if he went in.

"Please," she pleaded.

Inside, she held him tightly. "Oh, Eddie, let's do it before you go."

"Hey, we just did it before dinner," he said.

Kelly and Edgar

"I know, but...oh, Eddie, I love you so much. I miss you *so* when you are away. Please promise you'll come back."

"Come on," he said, "I promise. I'll see you for lunch, and I'll call you when I get to the office."

"Oh, Eddie—couldn't you stop by on your way?"

"Hey, I don't want to take a chance of waking you up. We both need some sleep or we'll collapse."

She put her lips on him—he pulled away. "Hey, you don't want this sore throat, believe me."

"If you have it," Kelly said, "I want it."

He gave her a chaste kiss—she held on for dear life. When he finally pulled away he saw she had tears in her eyes.

He waved goodbye from the car and she was crying nonstop.

As he drove toward Thousand Oaks and Penelope, he thought, I have finally found someone more insatiable than I. And, I hate to admit, it is knocking me out. I don't think I could have lived through another night with her. That's not saying I can look forward to a lot of peace from

Penelope. I expect she'll be haranguing me all night about my "bimbo." Well, I'd just better let her know that my so-called bimbo has given me more pleasure in these few weeks than my Ph.D. wife has in thirty-five years.

Suddenly Edgar had a blinding headache. He pulled off the freeway onto the gravelly shoulder, while his head pounded and his vision blurred. Finally it subsided and he carefully got back on the freeway.

Geez, he thought, if I want to live to see sixty, I'm going to have to slow down. I wonder where I ever got the idea I could keep up with a twenty-three-year-old?

PENELOPE

Edgar came home dragging. I wanted to say that should teach him to go fucking around with a twenty-three-year-old, but I held my tongue. He headed straight for the bedroom, so I followed him.

"How've you been, Edgar?" I said. "I've missed you."

He snorted as though I had just said something ridiculous.

"I'm really beat," he said.

"Well, let's go to bed," I said, then I added with a sultry twist, "I'm ready." He seemed startled. Like that was the last thing he wanted.

"I'm afraid..." he started to say, then stopped as if the words refused to form. He sat down on the bed without taking his clothes off. Next thing I knew he is laying back with his feet up, his shoes still on.

I realized, looking at him, that the thirty-five years of our relationship had taken its toll. I always said men and women are not compatible—that they want entirely different things—they look at things so differently. But now I realized that maybe it didn't apply to all men and women—at least not all the time. I could sense from looking at this gray shell of the man I married that he had found someone he was compatible with.

And then I wanted him like I never had before. It was as though some long-superfluous check valve had been released inside of me and it had been this mysterious mechanism that had held me back all these years. And wouldn't you know it would spring open too late to save me.

We all have different oestrus levels and

my threshold had been breached. Edgar, on the other hand, was a stone.

Oh, why must we always want what we can't have?

"Here, let me undress you," I said. He didn't resist. I took off his shoes and socks. He was docile by the time I got to his shirt and pants. He rolled over so I could get him under the covers, but he could do little else.

Looking at him helplessly nude, I was suddenly transported back to our first time. It was the wedding night, of course, neither of us were big drinkers, but at the wedding reception we were social, of course — it was *our* wedding. Apparently we were more social than we realized. We got to bed and started some fumbling when I excused myself to go to the bathroom to prepare for the fertility onslaught with my anti-fertility device. When I got back to bed Edgar was asleep.

And, you know, I was actually a little disappointed. But everything came out all right in the morning. I always wondered if that wasn't a metaphor for our marriage. I have never mentioned that to a living soul. I must have forgotten it. But now, in this crisis, I am remembering a lot of things I hadn't thought about in decades.

Now, after thirty-five years, it was the next morning again.

I undressed and crawled in with him. I ran my fingers lightly up and down his back. His flesh was warm. He didn't seem to have the energy to resist. I moved closer, then he muttered, "I'm pretty shot."

I could just imagine. I began to fondle. He twitched. "I've got a terrible sore throat," he said. "I don't want you to catch it."

"That's okay," I said. "You may have noticed I don't kiss."

I persevered, but it was no use. There was no juice left in the old grapefruit, and you know what they say: You can't get honey from lemons.

"Do you want to talk?" I asked him.

"No," he said.

"Well, I do."

"I'm half asleep, and really shot."

"I'm sorry about that," I said. "But I haven't seen you in a week. *Carpe diem*. What do you want," I pressed, "a divorce?"

"If that's what it takes to let me go to sleep."

I got nowhere. He was asleep, while I tossed and turned. I must have finally gotten some sleep, because I awoke to find his arm thrown across my chest. It had red blotches on it.

Good Lord, I thought at first, he's got the measles. Then I thought he might have picked up some venereal disease. Carefully, I removed his arm.

I looked at the bedside clock. It was six-thirty. I noticed Edgar was perspiring and it wasn't that hot. I put my palm on his forehead. He was burning up. I didn't want to wake him, and I should have gotten ready for work, but I didn't want to desert him either. He didn't look good.

Suddenly he started to moan.

"Edgar, are you all right?"

"What time is it?" he asked. He was so groggy I could hardly understand him.

Then when he tried to get up he collapsed on the floor. I shrieked—I ascertained he was breathing and I called the paramedics.

All I could think of was, no wonder, he's almost sixty years old and that bimbo has absolutely worn him out.

And wouldn't you know it, when he came to in the hospital, all he could talk about was the bimbo. By that time they had done their tests and hooked him up to the requisite life supports.

Around two in the afternoon he opened his eyes and tried to focus on where he was and what was happening to him.

Well, you know who he asked for as soon as he found his voice. "Kelly, where's my Kelly?"

I tried to calm him. To explain what happened to him, probably as a result of an overdose of Kelly.

"Call her," he said. "Tell her where I am."

"Now, Edgar," I tried to soothe him. I was no medical doctor, but I could tell it was not good for him to get so agitated.

Finally, I agreed to call her. He gave me the number. He had it memorized. Naturally.

I went to seek out the pay phone on the floor.

To tell the truth, I seriously considered lying to Edgar about calling. I could say she didn't answer, or the phone was out of order, but he would probably just insist I go after her then. I didn't know he'd gotten her an apartment in Santa Barbara. Pretty big-time stuff for such a modest man, if you ask me.

So I dialed her number and she snatched the phone up before it had completed one ring.

"Eddie?" this frantic voice pleaded on the phone. All I could think of was, my God, she calls him "Eddie"!

"Eddie," she called out again, as if in a heartrending search for a lost child. "Eddie, is that you? Say it's you, oh, please."

I wanted to say I had a wrong number and hang up, but I knew there would be no peace from "Eddie" if I did.

"No," I started slowly. "Edgar is in the hospital."

"Oh, my God—NO!" she shouted. "Is he all right?"

"Well, you don't go to hospitals if you are all right," I said. "He's alive, if that's what you mean."

"Oh, thank God. What happened?"

"He passed out this morning."

She groaned.

"Headache, sore throat, fever and red spots."

"It's...nothing...serious...is...it?" she asked one word at a time.

"The doctors are still evaluating the tests."

"Where is he?"

"Well, I don't know if you…"

The Real Sleeper

"Can I come over?"

"I don't think that's a good…"

"Is he in a room where I can see him?"

"Yes," I surrendered. "Mercy Hospital," I said, and gave her the address. I prided myself on being a large-spirited woman.

She hung up on a "Thanks," for which I was grateful. She hadn't even asked who I was. But then I expect she knew.

KELLY AND EDGAR

Kelly arrived at the hospital in under an hour and dashed to Edgar's room, then took in the scene with the tubes and wires and sank to her knees beside the bed.

"Oh, Eddie," she cried.

"Thanks for coming," he said.

"Thanks for having me," she said. Kelly wasn't paying any attention to the tallish woman at the door who now cleared her throat and said—"If you need anything, I'll be outside." And the tall woman slipped behind the door and vanished into the hall.

"Who was that?" Kelly asked.

"That's Penelope."

"Who's Penelope?"

"My wife."

Kelly reached over to take his hand. "Oh, Eddie, I'm your wife now."

He smiled and patted her hand weakly.

"But what's happened, Eddie? Why are you in here? Are you real bad? What are all these pipes and stuff? When can you get out?"

"Lot of questions." He smiled a thin, white smile.

"You don't have to answer them if you are too weak."

But he could still hoist those thin lips into a smile. "I'm so sorry I was late—didn't call—unconscious." He squeezed her hand with all his waning strength.

"Oh, Eddie, don't worry—you'll be out of here in no time, then we'll just pick up where we left off."

"Oh, I hope so," Edgar said. "But I'm afraid, Kelly."

Kelly and Edgar

"Afraid of what, Eddie?"

"Afraid I'm going to be the real sleeper. Afraid I...I...might...die." It wasn't easy for him to grip and share the thought.

"Well, gosh, yes, we're all going to die, but you aren't going soon."

In spite of her optimistic encouragement, Edgar said, "Life certainly can take cruel turns. Just when I've had my first real reason to live, I'm afraid I might just go to sleep, and never wake up."

"Eddie!" she scolded. "You know our rule about downer talk."

"I'm so glad I didn't put off calling you for that first dinner any longer. If I waited till I felt like this, it never would have happened." Edgar spoke in a hoarse whisper. His throat was burning.

"Well, I'm glad too, yes, I am," she said. "Now, you just get well because we have a lot of books to talk about. I've been reading, you know, because I want you to finally put some smarts in my dumb head."

Edgar moved his head to the side. "You're not dumb, Kelly."

It was *so* cruelly unfair.

The Real Sleeper

Perhaps there *was* a God and he was saying, "Enough already." Maybe Edgar had been blessed to pack so much sensual ecstasy into so short a time. Maybe your life span was in inverse proportion to your accomplishment. Look at Mozart. Edgar had twenty-five years on him already. And look what the kid packed into his thirty-five years. Schubert, Mendelssohn, Keats. Ah, but then there were the old men like Bach and Einstein, Picasso and Shaw. No, Edgar decided, it was all genetics after all. All the same, he was so grateful he hadn't put it off—this passion he shared with Kelly. It would give him a searing memory to the end.

PENELOPE

Well, it's official. Edgar has cancer. Cancer of the blood—leukemia. Starts in the bone marrow and once it's out, your luck is out too.

I haven't told Edgar or the bimbo, but the doctor told me he could go very quickly.

I do feel sorry for him, but I am more than a little pissed off he wants to spend so much time with the bimbo. She never leaves his side except to go to the bathroom. She shares his meals, and when I came in this morning, she was in bed with him. Imagine! Oh, they weren't doing anything, there was no question of that, but it's so damn unseemly.

At a time like this, he belongs with his wife of thirty-five years. Not for appearances, but because I understand him and can better minister to his needs. What is sex next to that? Not that he'll ever be able to perform again.

But the worst goddamned thing is I've gone all mushy inside for the big dying twerp. Like I was the empty-headed twenty-three-year-old bimbo. My goddamned eyes are watering just thinking about it. Did it take the competition to bring this out of me? I don't know, but I'd just as soon sublimate it again.

Maybe if Edgar had gotten regular checkups the big C could have been checked. But in life there are always a lot of maybes.

So you can just imagine how awkward it is for us—the three of us, I mean—in the room at the same time. It's obvious I'm the third wheel. So I leave them alone a lot of the time. Catch up on my work. I wasn't cut out to be a nursemaid anyway. I don't know about Bimbo. She doesn't seem to mind. It is strange watching your dying husband of thirty-five years so in love with someone else. All the same, I wish Edgar had given some sign he wanted *me* to be the nursemaid. I'd have given up *everything*.

Then, right in the midst of all this tension and uncertainty, Edgar says he wants Kelly to have his share of our estate if he doesn't make it.

We both pooh-poohed that; the bimbo, I must tell you, with a little more vehemence than I, but that I ascribed to our age gap, not to mention my inside knowledge of his fate.

When you are young, it is so much easier to place hope over experience.

The bimbo did have the grace to insist she didn't want his money, only him. Imagine! And she made a fairly convincing show of it, I must say. How charmingly old-fashioned. The next thing you know I am scurrying around to find him a lawyer to write a will.

Well, I found one. James Barker was his name, if I remember right, and he was awfully stuffy for his tender years. The dew of his graduation was still behind his ears, and to look at him was to cast serious doubt on the salubriousness of his diet. Stuffy and Puffy I called him: James J.

Barker from the august firm of Stuffy and Puffy. Firm nothing, J. J. was a solo practioner, selected in a telephonic competitive-bidding contest. J. J. was, as they say, the low bidder. He even came in a dark blue, pin-striped suit with a plain white shirt and plain navy tie. J. J. Barker was, you could say, vanilla.

His first act of kindness on entering Edgar's hospital room was to digest the interests of the *ménage à trois*, then banish the women to the hallway so he might get an unbiased take on the thing. Much as I hated to be in the hall with the bimbo, I thought that showed an unusual sensitivity on the part of our young barrister.

But it was some experience being alone with Bimbo. We both realized we could have fled to the bathroom or cafeteria, but that would have been like admitting defeat, like forfeiting our visitation rights to the other, so we simply stared at the floor and stole furtive glances at each other. To her credit, she spoke first.

"I love him so much," she said in this pathetic tone of her syrupy Southern voice. "If anything happens to him I will just *die*."

I was too stunned to answer—or too out of joint, I don't know which.

"I guess this is hard on you, huh?" she asked with a naiveté I was starting to find engaging. While she was certainly no rocket scientist, she did seem to have good instincts. I found I could understand how Edgar could find that combination of stupidity and horse sense appealing.

One thing my formidable age has taught me is that it is a lot easier to despise someone in the abstract than in actual face-to-face combat. Meeting people invariably softens you to them. You sense more your common humanity. I mean, here is a real person I've been calling a bimbo all these severely trying weeks. Then I meet her and see she is just pretty much like the rest of us—two eyes, ears, a nose, mouth and womb. It's a lot harder to hold the grudge. And the amazing thing is, a true-blue bimbo would have checked out of this thing at the first sight of blood. "So long, sweetie, got to go for an interview," she could have easily said. But she didn't.

Now I don't mean to suggest she won me over completely, or anything close to it. I'm nothing if not a tough old broad, but I confess to some softening. Sympathy, you might say.

It's funny when you think about it. Set us

side by side—this young beauty and I—and no one would look at me. Yet in any kind of intelligence test she would be left at the starting gate, where everybody, men and women alike, would still be looking at her.

So, early on, these young beauties get used to admiration and adulation, for nothing more substantial than how they look, which was no doing of their own in the first place.

Yet, it seems that the guys they'd like are put off from approaching them for some reason or other. Edgar certainly would have been, had he not met Kelly in the flesh, so to speak.

The guys who hit on them are not every woman's dream, but, so much of life is wanting what you can't have.

Well, Stuffy Puffy Barker wrote Edgar's will in time for him to sign it, with a nurse as witness. I am mentioned in passing as a "beloved wife," but the real tangible assets went to Kelly O'Leary. The real beloved, albeit short-term.

Pretty expensive screwing, I'd say, but so much of life is timing.

My own attorney has suggested I might be in a good position to contest the will. I certainly considered it. Logic and reason were way over on my side, but finally I thought, what the hell, if that's what he wants. He didn't have much in his life and she won't get all that much on his death, but we can let him have that one, small, last decision.

At least I'll get his gawd-awful paintings out of the house, and she's welcome to them. Well, I don't know, maybe, between us, I might keep just one. I don't think Kelly would begrudge me that.

The next thing I knew, Kelly was reading by Edgar's bedside. Edgar was asleep.

"What are you reading?" I asked. There was no sense being uncordial to her. She was a reality by now.

"*Anna Karenina*," she said, and started to spew forth her enthusiasm for the book, and I can't explain it, but I actually found myself liking her in that guise.

Then she asked the question I dreaded.

"Have you read it?"

And, I had to admit, I hadn't.

EDGAR AND KELLY

The secret was out. Without anyone ever having to tell them, both Edgar and, more reluctantly, Kelly got the message.

Edgar was so drawn, wan and weak that it would have taken an enormous leap of faith for anyone to not recognize what was happening.

Kelly never acknowledged it verbally. She had this peculiar feeling that if she did, it would hasten the reality.

She was lying beside Edgar in his hospital bed. But she was not as brave as she would have liked to have been. Sometimes, for no apparent reason, she would break down and the tears would flow unstaunched. Then Edgar would pat her wordlessly, for the patting alone was taking all his strength now.

Edgar was so weak he was unaware of his surroundings except for the feel of Kelly next to him. His sight was gone, his hearing faded and his ability to speak, strained.

"It's so cruel," Kelly said, crying openly.

"Hm?"

"You being sick. You're the finest person I know. It's not fair," she sniffled. "It's cruel."

"Maybe not so cruel," Edgar whispered. "Old man, healthy, sensual young woman. How much longer?"

"Forever!" Kelly insisted. "And after that I'll be right with you in heaven or hell or wherever you decide to go."

"You are worth one thousand years."

"Is that all?" Kelly said with her impish smile; that crazy, simple smile that Edgar visualized and would gladly die for. "You mean a lot more than that to me." She tapped his nose with her forefinger. "You are just my whole life, is all, my whole self. I wasn't even a person till I met you. Now I'm even reading *books*! You are the first person who ever made me feel worthwhile. Not just a pretty face and a cute behind. I used to have to take my clothes off to be admired, but now I feel admired even when I'm alone—and it's all thanks to you. You know, I now know all life is within, and since you were within me, you always will be. I feel you inside of me always, Eddie. No one will ever take that from me. I always had this inferiority thing. Now I think I could do anything—even nine to five. And it's all because of you. You aren't *only* the best thing that ever happened to me, you are the best thing that *could* ever happen to *anybody*!"

She stood and bent over him, choking on her tears, took him in her arms and gave him the best hug he ever had in his life. It made him feel as if he were already in the bosom of an angel.

And then he was.